THE LOST THINGS CLUB

J. S. PULLER

LITTLE, BROWN AND COMPANY

New York Boston

Little, Brown and Company
Hachette Book Group
1290 Avenue of the Americas, New York, NY 10104
Visit us at LBYR.com

First Edition: August 2021

Little, Brown and Company is a division of Hachette Book Group, Inc. The Little, Brown name and logo are trademarks of Hachette Book Group, Inc.

The publisher is not responsible for websites (or their content) that are not owned by the publisher.

Library of Congress Cataloging-in-Publication Data
Names: Puller, J. S., author.
Title: The Lost Things Club / J. S. Puller.
Description: First edition. | New York : Little, Brown and Company, 2021. | Audience: Ages 8–12. | Summary: Visiting her lovable younger cousin in Chicago over the summer, twelve-year-old Leah tries to help him recover from the trauma of a school shooting.
Identifiers: LCCN 2020030153 | ISBN 9780759556133 (hardcover) | ISBN 9780759556102 (ebook) | ISBN 9780759553903 (ebook other)
Subjects: CYAC: Cousins—Fiction. | Post-traumatic stress disorder—Fiction | School shootings—Fiction. | Jews—United States—Fiction. | Chicago (Ill.)—Fiction.
Classification: LCC PZ7.1.P787 Lo 2021 | DDC [Fic]—dc23
LC record available at https://lccn.loc.gov/2020030153

ISBNs: 978-0-7595-5613-3 (hardcover), 978-0-7595-5610-2 (ebook)

Printed in the United States of America

LSC-C

Printing 1, 2021

To: Doctor Stephanie Kaplan
From: Your Loyal Companion
Thank you for all the childhood adventures!

CHAPTER ONE

I was lost.

There are lots of different kinds of ways to be lost. I don't mean to say that I didn't know where I was. I knew exactly where I was: sitting in the back seat of my mom's silver Chevy Impala, cruising south on I-94, past billboards with splashy logos and smiling faces. And it wasn't like I'd forgotten who I was or where I was going. I was Leah Abramowitz, a brown-haired, brown-eyed lump of a girl, heading down to Chicago from my home in Deerwood Park, about an hour north.

This was a new kind of lost.

The kind that left me antsy, fidgeting in my seat, inventing new ways to keep myself busy.

He isn't talking.

I had already looked up several websites that were posted on the billboards we passed, just to figure out what they were. A country-western radio station, a touring Broadway musical, and a customized car-mat service, for the record. Staring out the front windshield, between the headrests, I held up my phone and took a picture of the Chicago skyline. It was like a jagged row of teeth, biting a perfect blue sky. I studied the picture, my eye drawn to one of the smaller skyscrapers; it looked like some kind of crystal, with its corners sliced off, a sloping, smooth diamond on the top, catching the sunlight.

What was that place?

Did amazing and wonderful things happen there?

I opened a browser on my phone and typed "chicago building diamond shaped top" into the search bar.

The Crain Communications Building.

A picture of the building came up immediately, along with a link to the Wikipedia page. I clicked on it and tried to read, but the text on the page blurred in front of my eyes.

He isn't talking.

I heard the words again and again in my head.

I closed Wikipedia.

Next, I opened up an app that let me fit together the pieces of a virtual puzzle. This one was a picture of a beautiful hiking trail. The kind where lost campers met up with the monster with a chain saw in the first five minutes of a horror movie. I could usually put puzzles together in my sleep, but after sliding all the edge pieces to one side of the screen, I gave up and closed the app.

I just wasn't in the mood.

Maybe I could play some music?

But my earbuds were in the trunk, at the bottom of one of my duffel bags.

Check my email?

I'd already done that twice.

Update my apps?

Everything was already up-to-date.

Anyway, they were all just excuses to ignore the reality of my situation.

We were getting closer.

Closer to the apartment where Uncle Toby and Aunt Lisa lived.

With TJ.

He isn't talking.

TJ was my cousin, named after Uncle Toby, because Aunt Lisa insisted. Toby Isaac Cantor Jr. A mouthful for such a small kid, not even eight years old, who still asked me to check under his bed for monsters when he slept over at our apartment, up in Deerwood Park. "TJ" felt more appropriate, somehow. Two little taps on the keypad. Two beeps. Little noises for a little boy.

A little boy who wasn't himself.

"He isn't talking," my mom warned me, as I packed my duffel bags for the three weeks I was spending in Chicago.

"What do you mean, 'isn't talking'?" I asked her. I knew TJ. Sometimes, it was impossible to get him to shut up. Aunt Lisa was an English teacher, and she'd had TJ reading and writing practically the moment he was born. Every day, she insisted, he had to write a hundred words. And read for at least half an hour. He knew words that I didn't even know. Words like "omnipotent" and "obfuscate" and "octogenarian." Words I had to look up after, while pretending I knew exactly what they meant in the moment. He went through books so fast that he was visiting the library once a week, at least, always coming back with his arms—and Aunt Lisa's tablet—loaded, his eyes gleaming brighter than silver coins as he admired the covers with their bright, colorful characters. He gave me long, thoughtful book reports about all of them, even though I kept telling him that I wasn't his teacher and he didn't have to.

"I mean not talking," my mom replied, leaning against the doorframe. "Uncle Toby says not a single word."

"How is that possible?"

She didn't have an answer for me. And I think that was part of what was scaring me.

I liked answers.

I liked them a lot.

Every July, while my mom traveled out of the country for work with her boss and her boss's boss, I spent three weeks with Uncle Toby, Aunt Lisa, and TJ. Those three weeks were always the best weeks of the year. We'd visit museums and go to concerts in Millennium Park. See plays. Ride the Ferris wheel at Navy Pier. Take long, lazy walks along the shore of Lake Michigan. Make faces at the fish in the aquarium. Have all kinds of adventures. Tell each other silly stories until we fell asleep laughing.

But TJ wasn't talking.

Which meant this summer wasn't going to be like other summers in Chicago.

I had the sinking suspicion that there wouldn't be any adventures.

Or stories.

For the first time ever, I was beginning to dread getting there. Which, of course, meant we were there before I knew it.

But I swallowed my fear. I was always really good at hiding my feelings. I learned that if I let my feelings show, people usually bothered me about it. *Especially* teachers. I always hated it when Mr. Gardener, my third-grade teacher, asked me "How's life at home?" It was none of his business. So I learned to never look sad, and I never let myself cry, either. Not anymore. Not since my parents split when I was eight years old, and my dad moved away.

There weren't any skyscrapers or museums or monuments where Uncle Toby and Aunt Lisa lived. Technically, yes, their home was in Chicago. In a neighborhood called Oak Lake. But it was about as far from the excitement of downtown as you could get. The streets were evenly spaced, latticed like a piecrust. Along both sides of the car, there was nothing but town houses and trees. The occasional shop. And then more town houses and trees. The only clue that we were in the city at all was the rumbling of the elevated train lines, somewhere in the distance, hidden behind—you guessed it—town houses and trees.

The curbs were cluttered with parked cars. So many that we had to go around the block three times before my mom found a spot. We grabbed my duffel bags and walked to Uncle Toby and Aunt Lisa's front door. A buzzer let us in, and we climbed up the cement stairs, huffing and puffing the whole way.

"What did you pack in here, Leah?" my mom asked, trying to hoist the strap of a duffel up higher on her shoulder.

"Just stuff," I said.

Clothes. Shoes. A toothbrush. My laptop. My tablet. The tablet charger. My phone charger. Three external batteries. A portable keyboard. My Nintendo Switch and its charger. Nothing special.

Aunt Lisa was waiting on the third floor, in the doorway

to their apartment. She had tight bleached-blond curls that spiraled down to her shoulders, and she wore a pale pink dress, with little roses embroidered across the hem. She was so pretty. Like a picture. I quickly took out my phone and snapped one with the camera.

"Leah!" she said when she saw us, in her lilting Southern twang. "Oh, don't take any pictures of me, sweetheart! I'm a mess this morning."

Her idea of a mess was most people's idea of a classy magazine shoot. The photo looked great. She reached out and took the duffel bag from my mom, letting out a grunt of surprise. "Ooof, that's heavy. You planning on moving in, Leah?"

She always asked me that.

"So much *stuff*. She's turning into a teenager," my mom said. "*Twelve* now. I only have one year left until it happens!"

"Oh, teenagers aren't so bad. You just need to learn how to work with them. My students? Every year, they come in snarling like tigers. But by the end of the year, they're all just sweet little pussycats." Shaking her head, she ushered us inside. "Toby!" she shouted, calling down the hallway. "Toby! Get over here. Your sister is here with Leah." She turned back to my mom. "He's been in his study all morning, fiddling with this new gadget he picked up. It's some sort of drone."

I looked around the front room. We hadn't visited since

7

March, and it was July already. But it hadn't changed. It was in pristine condition, in fact. Picture-perfect. Just the way Aunt Lisa liked it. Not a speck of dust to be found. The same white-and-gray couch facing the TV. The same bookshelves, so tightly packed that the extra books were lying on the top in jagged piles. The same kitchen table, cluttered with papers and notebooks and whatever Aunt Lisa's latest summer project happened to be—she always had one, because she said it helped her not miss her students so much. But something felt... different. What was missing?

"Hello, hello," Uncle Toby said, coming in from the hallway. He was a large man, almost as round as he was tall. His hair had thinned into a dark ring around the base of his skull long ago, but his beard and mustache were still thick and black, with only the faintest hints of silver. He might have been intimidating, all that weight, all that power. Like a grizzly bear. But really, he was all marshmallow on the inside.

"Talking about my new drone? It's great. It reminds me of the spy drones we used in the CIA," he said, taking a sip from a bottle of orange pop—I almost never saw him without one.

Aunt Lisa swatted his side with the back of her hand. "Don't start with that again. You were never in the CIA, Toby."

"That's just what I want you to think," he said, his eyes shifting to me, like he was checking to see that I was listening. "If you knew my true identity, I'd be forced to erase your memories."

"And how would you do that?" Aunt Lisa asked.

He smiled absently, but it looked a little thin. "I fear I've said too much already."

"Probably fancy government nanotechnology," I said, pinching my fingers together. "Robots that are so bitty they crawl in through your ear and mess with your brain." I'd started reading Wikipedia pages and found one on nanotechnology a few days before. Really, I was happy to read any old page. I loved the "Random article" link. Every page I read was like a little treasure. Shining information. Part of the larger puzzle that was the world.

My favorite pages, though, were about people. I liked to figure out what made someone special enough to have their very own page.

Aunt Lisa huffed. "Sweetheart, I think if nanotechnology was able to do that, I would have used it on your uncle to reprogram his brain years ago."

"Now, that's just insult on top of injury," Uncle Toby said.

He walked over to give my mom a kiss on each cheek before leaning down to look at me, his hand on his knee. "How's my favorite Illinois niece?" he asked.

"Fine," I said.

"Why don't you get Leah settled in and show her that drone of yours?" Aunt Lisa said. She turned to my mom. "I'll bet you could use some coffee, Hannah."

My mom groaned happily. "Yes. Please."

"Come on," Aunt Lisa said, setting my duffel bag down on the floor. "I'll put on a fresh pot." And without warning, she snatched the bottle of pop out of Uncle Toby's hand. "And you. Healthy food from now on, remember? It's on Ms. Weinstein's list."

"*Hey,*" he said in annoyance.

"We're *all* going to follow everything on that list, Toby. *All* of us."

And with that, the two of them disappeared into the kitchen.

"That was harsh," I said, wondering who Ms. Weinstein was and why she was suddenly controlling Uncle Toby's diet.

"Good thing she doesn't know where I keep my secret stash," Uncle Toby said, picking up my bag with a grunt. "This way; we're putting you in the study this time. There's an air conditioner in the window, so you should be very comfortable."

Air-conditioning. I'd read that Wikipedia article a week before on a sweaty, humid morning when I went to work with my mom and she insisted on opening the windows instead of cranking the AC in the car. The article said there was evidence of primitive air-conditioning as far back as ancient Egypt.

It was pretty primitive here, too.

Uncle Toby and Aunt Lisa's building had been built decades ago, before central air-conditioning was a thing. The hallway was stifling, the heat swelling up the floorboards so they creaked and groaned with every step. I followed Uncle Toby, cringing at the noise. But when he passed TJ's room, I stopped and looked in through the doorway.

I felt something twist in my throat, like I'd swallowed a live goldfish. But I forced it down.

He isn't talking.

The bed in TJ's room was made.

It was neat. Impeccable, as a matter of fact.

TJ was sitting on it, at the corner where the bed met the wall. He had one of his pillows in his lap. And he was staring at it. I noticed that he didn't have any books open beside him.

"Hey, Hedgehog," I said, taking a step toward the threshold of the room, then taking a step back for some reason.

He looked up. TJ had the same chubby, round features as Uncle Toby, but he had Aunt Lisa's light coloring. His eyes were storm-cloud gray.

And there were heavy bags under those eyes that hadn't been there back in March. Deep purple.

He didn't say anything.

After a moment, he turned his attention back to the pillow on his lap. Just like that. Like I hadn't been there at all.

"Hedgehog?" I said.

This time, he didn't look up at all. Like he hadn't even heard me.

"TJ?"

Nothing.

"Hey. It's me. Your favorite Illinois cousin."

It hurt that he didn't respond. The kind of hurt I couldn't exactly describe, but one that cut deep into my soul.

Not that I let it show. If I wasn't going to cry in front of my third-grade teacher, you can bet I wasn't going to be caught dead crying in front of Uncle Toby.

Uncle Toby put a hand on my shoulder. I looked over at him, and he shook his head before gesturing for me to follow him.

So it was true. TJ wasn't talking. I found that I missed the sound of his voice. Usually, when I came to visit, TJ would come bounding into the front room the second he heard the buzzer. He'd be jumping around like a little acrobat.

"Leah! Leah! Come to my room! Read me a story! Read me a story!"

That was it.

That's what was missing when I first came into the apartment. The feeling that something was different.

There was no TJ.

No roly-poly Hedgehog.

The front room felt empty without him. Incomplete, somehow. Like a puzzle that was missing a piece.

Uncle Toby took me down the hall to the study. It was a crowded room with a large computer desk, a sleeper sofa, and a coffee table, currently covered with pieces of drone.

"He really isn't talking," I said, setting down my duffel bag by the sofa.

"No." Uncle Toby dropped the other duffel with a noisy rattle and took a seat on the sofa, sinking deep into the cushions with a sigh. "He just hasn't been the same since . . . well. I probably shouldn't talk about it."

He didn't have to talk about it.

I remembered the day of the shooting at TJ's school. It was March 24. A beautiful spring day. It happened around eleven o'clock in the morning. I was in my social studies class and bored to tears—who cared about the Battle of Gettysburg anymore?—so I snuck a peek at my phone.

As I scrolled around, a hashtag lit up social media: #ChancelorShooting.

At first, I thought it was a movie. You know. "Shooting" a movie.

But when I tapped on the hashtag, a horrifying headline popped up:

Reports of a Shooting at Chancelor Elementary School in Chicago

Chancelor Elementary School?

My heart started to beat faster. And a sharp panic started to rise before I clamped it down, like I was slamming a door in its face.

That was TJ's school.

The world was full of "oh, what a shame" and "not again" and "why does this keep happening?" when people heard the news. Or read it. Or tweeted it. Or texted it. It was all over the place, to the point where I had to put away my phone, turn off the TV, and hide in the bathroom just to get away from it.

I frowned a little bit, sitting next to Uncle Toby on the couch. "I don't get it. TJ's fine. He wasn't hurt."

That was a *fact*.

"No," Uncle Toby said. "He wasn't. But things have been rough since then."

"Why?"

He made a helpless gesture. "These things are tricky, Leah. I wish I had an answer, but I don't know. Something like that changes you," he said. "That's what Ms. Weinstein says."

The famous Ms. Weinstein who didn't like orange pop. "Who *is* Ms. Weinstein?" I asked.

"TJ's counselor."

"Counselor?"

"Like a doctor," Uncle Toby said. "But for your feelings."

"I *know* what a counselor is," I said, rolling my eyes. "Is she making him better?"

"To tell you the truth, I don't think he likes her very much."

"Why not?"

"Well, for one thing," Uncle Toby said, "he ran away from her office a few weeks ago."

I let out a laugh and quickly covered my mouth with both hands. It wasn't supposed to be funny. But the idea of TJ doing something like that was just ridiculous. He was so obedient. He was the sort of kid my mom wished I could be. Never argued. Never broke the rules. *Never* got sent to the principal's office.

"You're kidding."

"No," Uncle Toby said, scrubbing his face with the heels of his palms. "Not kidding."

"Did he say why?"

The words barely left my lips when I remembered:
He isn't talking.

I winced at my mistake.

"He won't tell his story. We don't know what happened. That day. To him." Uncle Toby stared out into the hallway. "He'll make a few noises here and there. Grunts and groans. But not much else. It's like we've lost him completely."

I didn't really know how to respond. How could I? "Oh," I said.

"I got this drone for him," Uncle Toby said, picking up two of the pieces and fiddling with them a bit. "All the books say that after something like this, it's important to try to keep a kid's routine as normal as possible. I thought he might have fun putting it together with me but..."

He tried to fit the pieces together, but they wouldn't interlock. Gently, I reached over and turned his hand. The joint came together with a satisfying click. Uncle Toby smiled. "Ah, my magical girl," he said.

I shrugged.

"I hope you're not going to be too bored with us while you're here."

And that confirmed it. What I'd been afraid of the whole car ride down to the city. I was right. There weren't going to be adventures. Not while TJ was lost.

Nothing was helping him.

But maybe... maybe I could?

We were so close, after all. Almost like brother and sister instead of cousins. I still remembered holding him in the hospital the day he was born. And I'd only been four! I hadn't seen him since the shooting, but maybe I could make the difference. I could be the missing piece. I liked the idea of helping. Because I loved him and because, well, maybe I really could be magical. *Special.*

The more I thought of it, the more it made sense. After all, I was great at dealing with emotions.

I didn't feel like I could say it, though. That I thought I could succeed where his parents were failing. So I just gave Uncle Toby a small smile. "As long as I have the internet, I can't get too bored."

He let out a hiccup of a laugh. "You find more ways to entertain yourself online than anyone I know." He gave me a kiss on the side of the head. "And in the meanwhile, you can help me with this drone. I'm completely lost. They don't make them like they used to, back in my FBI days."

"I thought it was the CIA."

"Well, I did a little side work for the FBI, on occasion."

"Oh, really?"

"Yes, really."

I hid another laugh behind my hand. "Uncle Toby..."

Smirking, he turned to look down at all the drone pieces. "I think these thingies"—he pointed to two long,

flat tongues of plastic that looked like propeller props—
"are supposed to fit in this." He picked up a small black
cylinder with two slots on either side.

I picked up the props and carefully started fitting them
into place. I didn't need directions. Technology was easy.
Everything just belonged a certain way. It made sense.
And after following a few basic steps, I had the propeller
spinning on my finger.

"Incredible," Uncle Toby said.

I liked the way he said that. As if I really was incredible.
I mean, I wanted to be. Who didn't want to be special?

The real question was if I was special enough to find a
way to get through to TJ. I had the whole world available
at my fingertips. My phone answered most of my questions. A quick search on the internet and I knew how to
catch fruit flies with apple cider vinegar, fix my hair in a
French braid, or beat the final boss in *The Legend of Zelda:
Link's Awakening*.

But I wasn't stupid. I knew that TJ was a little more
complicated than all those things.

There was a lot of searching in my future.

CHAPTER TWO

Word Fortune Predictor
The First Three Words You Spot
Will Tell Your Future!

It was a grid of random letters, twenty-five by twenty-five. I let my focus go soft, staring at the letters, and within a few seconds, I'd found my three words. They just seemed to jump out of the picture at me.

Journey

Surprises

Story

How did three words like that fit together? My future

was that I'd go on a journey full of surprises and live to tell the story? That seemed a little obvious. How could it be a journey if there *weren't* surprises? It sounded just like life.

Someone's life, anyway.

I wasn't sure it was really mine. It sometimes felt like nobody ever noticed me at school. There was nothing special about me, just another brown-eyed girl, trudging down the hall, hunched under the weight of my backpack. One of hundreds. And I *wanted* to be special. The problem was, I didn't know how to be. I was sure that there was some secret place where people went and they came back incredible. If only I could find a map; if only I could get there. No one knew I felt this way, except for Nicole.

Nicole was my best friend. She was away at summer theatre camp in Wisconsin. It was always weird being apart from her, since we saw each other every day during the school year. It felt like a part of me was missing. And I knew she felt the same way. So every morning, we would send each other a text about what we were up to. Today, she sent me a picture of herself in the costume storage closet. Nicole was wearing a cone-shaped hat with a long, flowing veil falling over her shoulder. A princess in a storybook. After the picture, she wrote:

> Think I can get away with wearing this to homeroom?

It made me laugh out loud.

I went scrolling through my camera roll, trying to find a picture to send her, but I hit the photos I'd taken last summer instead—selfies of me and TJ eating a giant ice cream sundae at the Ghirardelli store, pictures of me and TJ making goofy faces in front of Sue the T. rex at the Field Museum, blurry shots of me and TJ running to home base at a baseball diamond, the wide ribbon of Lake Shore Drive stretching out in the background behind us.

He isn't talking.

I sent Nicole the word fortune predictor instead.

There were no new pictures.

The change in TJ haunted me all night, as I lay awake on the lumpy sofa sleeper, listening to the air-conditioning unit sputter and shriek, thinking over my secret plan to try to help him come back to us. I wore down my phone battery searching for solutions.

I searched "not talking" first, but nothing useful came up. I tried "stopped talking" and "silent," too. I got some bands. A couple of books. A TV show. And a video game that my mom wouldn't let me play because she said I wasn't old enough. But nothing that seemed like TJ. After a while, I stumbled my way to a page about silent films... and I was lost along a trail of links again. I finally fell asleep with my face pressed up against the Wikipedia page about *Singin' in the Rain.*

Uncle Toby had already left for work by the time I was up and dressed, my poor, exhausted phone charging against the wall. Aunt Lisa was standing over the table in the living room, looking at a bunch of papers.

"Morning, Leah," she said, bouncing on the balls of her feet.

"Morning."

I walked over to the table and noticed a three-ring binder on the corner. It was open. On top was a sheet of paper with bold black print. The font was so small, the words looked like ants crawling across the page. I leaned over to take a peek. Scrawled across the header was a logo for the American School Counselor Association. Beneath, it read:

Helping kids after a school shooting

There was a numbered list below. Just like Uncle Toby said, right at the top, "Keep routines as normal as possible."

I flipped the page and found another printout, this one from the American Psychological Association. Just as black-and-white and boring:

Helping your children manage distress in the aftermath of a shooting

Another list. This one longer than the first.

Each page was another printout from another association of some kind. Most of them had impressively long
titles. I paused to scan one from the office of Jenny Weinstein. "Use simple words," it advised. "Children don't
understand phrases like 'passed away' or 'lost' or 'in a better place.'"

"Leah!"

I looked up, feeling my eyes widen. Aunt Lisa didn't
raise her voice often.

"What are you doing?"

"I was just looking at—"

"No, no," she said, leaning over to close the binder with
a heavy snap that nearly took a couple of my fingers off.
"Don't look at that. It's not for you."

"Sorry."

Her lips pressed together, forming a tight line for a
moment. At last, she sighed, shaking her head so that her
curls bounced against one another. "It's all right," she
said, her voice gentler but still kind of tense. She picked
up the binder, like she didn't trust me near it, and walked
across the room, tucking it into a cabinet. Her eyes cut
to one side, staring down the long, narrow hallway of the
apartment. The door to TJ's room was open. There were
no sounds coming from inside.

He isn't talking.

But he was in there. I could feel it.

I reached over and touched Aunt Lisa's elbow. "I'll go see how he's doing," I told her softly.

Aunt Lisa looked up at me, a whisper of a smile passing over her lips before it disappeared. "You're a sweetheart, Leah. But no. Leave him be. He doesn't want to talk."

"No, really," I said. "I could go—"

"Leave him be."

But how could I help him if I couldn't get near him?

"Why don't you go outside?" She waved at the window. "There are plenty of kids in the neighborhood. Maybe you can make some friends. Just stay between Keating and Downey."

"I don't know...."

"Go on. Go outside. It's a beautiful day."

"Okay."

"The code to let yourself back into the building is—"

"One-seven-zero-one," I cut her off. The code hadn't changed in years.

Aunt Lisa nodded. "Just buzz yourself back in when you're ready. You have fun."

Before I left, I went to the bathroom and attached two blond hair extensions to either side of my head. I wanted to dye my hair for real, but Mom wouldn't let me. She said I

24

was too young. But I'd managed to convince her to order a couple of fake curls that I could fix in my hair with pins. I guess I was kind of nervous. I mean, I didn't know anyone in Oak Lake. At all. My summer visits were usually dedicated to TJ, and without him—or Nicole—I felt a little . . . lost.

Aunt Lisa was right. There *were* a lot of kids on the block.

It was like the first day of school!

Cliques everywhere.

There was a group just across the street, sitting around an inflatable swimming pool. They looked a lot younger than I was and were busy splashing one another, flailing around in the water, ripping up the grass as they slipped and tripped away from one another.

I had a feeling we wouldn't have much in common.

A little bit farther up the block, where it opened to a stone alley between apartment buildings, a group of teenagers were kicking a soccer ball. They weren't playing a game. Just messing around. But even messing around, they had a certain grace and skill that I knew I lacked. One girl kicked up the ball with the tips of her toes and then started bouncing it, again and again, on her forehead. She moved in time with it. Like a dance. The other kids were getting into it, counting out loud with each bounce.

Not for me.

Soccer was just something you were forced to do in gym class.

I started to walk along the sidewalk, digging out my phone. I was desperate for a message from Nicole. I knew she was probably memorizing her lines or learning choreography or whatever it was that future superstars did, but I wished she was standing beside me. I needed someone to talk to. I sent her a text:

I miss your face. What are you up to?

But there was no reply.

It seemed to be the theme of my summer so far.

He isn't talking.

Okay, it was Wikipedia time.

I opened the home page, choosing "Random article."

I got a page about some weird Olympic event called curling. Just my luck. A sports page.

This really wasn't my day.

As I walked, I noticed a small gap between the parked cars. It was about big enough for another car. But instead, there was a girl with long brown hair, evenly divided into two braids, sitting in a lawn chair, leaning dangerously far away from the bumper of one of the cars. She was skinny. The kind of skinny that made her elbows and knees look like enormous knobs. One foot was crossed over the other, both heels propped up on the nearest car's exhaust pipe, and on her lap, she had a notebook. She was scribbling notes with a ballpoint pen.

The sight was just too bizarre. And in that moment, I figured I'd found my picture to send Nicole in the morning. But when I held out my phone, opening the camera app, I heard a voice. "It's rude to take pictures of people on the street without their permission."

It was the girl.

Guiltily, I slipped my phone into my back pocket. "What are you writing?" I asked her as I approached.

She looked up at me, and I was immediately struck by her eyes. They were an electric sort of blue, which I could best describe as the color of the computer screen of death. That moment right before a crash, when you still had hope that everything would be all right.

"Lists," she replied. There was a flash of silver in her mouth. The top row of her teeth had metal braces, with little purple rubber bands in front of each tooth. She had a stern voice. Matter-of-fact. Decisive. And, as I quickly learned, incredibly rapid. "The clubs I'm planning to join and the service projects I'm going to propose when school starts. You have to write to-do lists if you want to get anything done. Everyone says, 'Oh, I'll remember it later.' But they never do. So it never gets done. And what's the point of that?"

"Oh, I get it," I said. A pause. "I guess."

"And it's going to be a long time before I can even get around to doing anything on my lists," she continued. "School doesn't start again for *ages*. And I don't want to be that girl who gets left out of clubs because she doesn't remember to fill out all the applications in the first week. You know?"

Did I know? I auditioned for the school play last year, so I could be with Nicole, but my singing was about as beautiful as a car running over an aluminum can, so I wasn't cast. I didn't even bother trying out for any of the sports teams, either. I knew I wasn't good enough. I went to Hebrew school twice a week, but that wasn't by choice. My mom made me. In fact, the only club I had actually joined on my own was the quiz bowl. I was pretty good. I guess it was all the Wikipedia searches. No applications, though. The quiz bowl was probably just too desperate for members to bother.

"Why are you sitting in the street?" I asked, figuring it was best to change the subject before she realized I was lost.

"It's my father's spot," she said. "He called dibs. I'm just saving it for him."

"With a lawn chair?"

"Well, what else am I supposed to sit on? The ground? That's a one-way ticket to the ER for sure. Have you *seen* the way Chicago people drive?"

I shrugged. "Do you have to sit out here? Couldn't you just leave a sign or something that says dibs?"

She chuckled. "A sign? That's adorable. No one pays attention to *signs*," she said. "You have to enforce dibs, otherwise, you lose it. My uncle Al guards his spot with a baseball bat, but my mother won't let me. Going on and on about it being illegal or something." She raised both eyebrows, shaking her head.

"Oh."

"So what school do you go to?"

I had no idea where the question came from, and it took me a second to remember anything about myself at all. "Uh, Kohn Junior High."

"Never heard of it."

"It's in Deerwood Park."

"Oh. The *suburbs*." She said it as if, somehow, that explained everything about me. And maybe it did. "You must be TJ's cousin."

I blinked in surprise. "Yeah. How'd you know?"

"I saw you arrive yesterday." Her gaze darkened for a moment. "The lady driving your car tried to take this spot. But my father called dibs. I set her straight about that."

Now that I thought about it, I vaguely remembered my mom almost pulling into a spot. But I'd been on my phone and hadn't seen this strange girl sitting there.

My mom wasn't easily intimidated.

But this girl just might be the exception to the rule.

I held up my hands in a gesture of surrender. I didn't really care where my mom parked. The girl seemed to accept that, because the darkness lifted and she gave me a smile. That felt like an invitation, so I came closer. She smelled of sunscreen and something else, something sweet. Like one of those bear-shaped bottles of honey they kept in the kitchen at my mom's office.

"You know TJ?" I asked.

"Sure," she said. "I live right across the street from your aunt and uncle." She pointed to a town house on the opposite side of the street, with a redbrick facade and a crooked iron gate. "And TJ and I go to the same school."

"Chancelor?"

"Yeah. I see him sometimes in the hallways. He was in Mr. Hiler's class. Ms. Berns the year before that. I had both of them when I was a kid. He's reading buddies with my best friend, Samantha. Or, he was, anyway. And I'm pretty sure he was in gardening club last year. I was only a regular member then, but now I'm a vice president and I'm hoping to be president next year."

President? Somehow, I got the impression that she would make a very powerful and iron-fisted dictator.

"What grade are you in?" I asked her.

"Going to be in seventh grade when school starts up again."

Like me.

"Why aren't you in middle school?"

"We don't *have* middle schools in Chicago," she replied. "Our schools go all the way through eighth grade. Then we get to apply to high school. I'm already trying to decide which high school I want to go to. I mean, the selective enrollment schools are great, but personally, I think I'd rather go to an IB school. A couple of schools around here offer an International Baccalaureate Diploma Programme. They're really competitive. Colleges like them. And I appreciate the service element that goes into the diploma. My favorite program is definitely—"

"Do you like it?" I asked. "Not having a middle school? Being stuck in the elementary school with the little kids?"

She shrugged. "It's fine, I guess." She hooked her pen into the spiral of her notebook and then reached up above her head with her long, spindly arms, stretching out to her fullest length.

"My name's Violet," she told me. "Violet Kowalski." She held out her hand. It was a very, very formal posture. I'd sometimes practiced handshakes with my mom, when she introduced me to the people she worked with at the university, but never with someone my age before. But Violet's hand just hung there, waiting for me.

Oh, this was awkward.

"You shake hands?" I asked.

31

"Of course. It's excellent practice for job interviews."

"What?"

"Jooooooooooob interviiiiiiiiiiiieeeeeeews," Violet said, drawing out the words.

"You go on job interviews?"

"Well, not yet. But I will, someday. I mean, I plan to have a job. And you have to be prepared for the future. The handshake is everything. Too limp and no one takes you seriously. Too firm and people think that you're trying to prove something, which, of course, you are, but you can't let them know that."

"Oh."

What could I do?

I shook her hand.

Her fingers were like steel, the bony knobs of her knuckles digging into my skin.

"My name's Leah Abramowitz," I said.

"Leia? Like the princess from *Star Wars*?"

"No." I groaned inwardly because I got that all the time. My dad actually did want to name me after the *Star Wars* character, but my grandmother insisted that he give me a traditional Jewish name. She also wanted him to follow custom and name me after a deceased relative—specifically my great-aunt Emily. They ended up compromising, and I became Leah Emily instead. "Leah."

Violet nodded curtly. "Nice to meet you. Say it again."

I blinked. "What?"

"Saaaaaaaaaay iiiiiiiiiiiiit agaaaaaaaaain. Your name. Let me hear it."

"Leah Abramowitz?"

"Slower."

"Leeeee—"

"Leeeee—"

"Uhhhh."

"Leeeee-uhhhh. Leah Abramowitz," she said. She spoke carefully, copying the sound of each syllable. "Is that right?"

"Yeah," I said.

"Good. It's important to get someone's name right the first time. It proves that you're listening and that you take an interest in what they have to say. And it earns you respect in formal environments."

"Uh, thanks, I guess." I was beginning to get the sense that Violet had a lot of rules buzzing around inside her head, like bees in a hive. "Do you sit out in this spot every day?"

"Mostly just in the summer," she said. "I mean, I go to school when there's school to go to."

She sounded just like TJ. Or, well, how TJ usually sounded. He loved school. He would go on and on about his favorite lessons and friends and books.

He isn't talking.

And I wasn't exactly helping him, all the way out here. But maybe I had an opportunity staring me in the face.

I frowned a little, lowering my voice. "Hey," I said to Violet, "were you in Chancelor the day that..."

"The shooting?" Violet asked.

"Yeah."

She nodded. "But the sixth graders were in the middle-grades hall," she said. "The shooting happened on the other end of the building, in the elementary wing."

"Elementary wing?"

"Yeah."

I felt fear rise up inside me and had to force it down my throat. No fear allowed. "Is that where TJ would have—"

"His classroom was there, yeah," Violet said. "But if you're asking if he was there, he wasn't. He was in the principal's office when it happened."

"The principal's office?"

"Priiiiiiinciiiiipaaaaaaaaaal's offffffffiiiiiiiiice. That's what I said."

"But why?"

Violet shrugged. "He got into trouble for fighting."

Trouble? Fighting? "That doesn't sound like TJ."

"True," Violet said. "I mean, I've known him his whole life, practically. He's such a sweet kid. Really. But it's a lucky thing he was there. I mean, it was probably the safest part of the building."

I smiled a little bit. "It's not often that you're lucky to be in the principal's office. Last time I went there, my mom grounded me for a week."

"What did you do?"

"Checked my email during science class."

Violet snorted.

"What was it like?" I asked. "The shooting." I knew it was probably an inappropriate question, but I couldn't really help myself. You didn't get to hear the story first-hand often. It was always filtered through the news and the internet and people's loud opinions. Violet, though, seemed...direct. And not at all filtered. If I could ask anyone—if I could get the straight facts from anyone—it would have to be her. "What was it like?"

"Scary, I guess," she said. For the first time, there was a slight sense of softness in her voice. She'd slipped back into the memory of the day. I guess she was human after all. "I remember it was really quiet. And then, there was this announcement on the PA about how we had to shelter in place."

"What does that mean?"

"Squat down against the wall with the lights out and the door locked. And just kind of wait."

"For what?"

"For the police to tell us to leave the building."

"That's it?"

"That's it."

"That...doesn't sound so bad," I said.

"Well, not for us, it wasn't." Violet's voice dropped to a hiss, and she leaned closer to me. "But you know, we lost a kid."

"Lost?"

"He died. A few hours after they rushed him to the hospital."

My eyes widened. "I didn't know that." And I should have, too. Why hadn't I searched for the shooting online?

Violet nodded. "I didn't know him personally—his family had just moved into the neighborhood—but we heard about it. We all heard about it. There was a candlelight vigil down the street. Almost every family in the school was there, and Star Williamson's father brought cookies with *peanut butter* in them. And Camilla Goelz's mother asked what he was thinking, was he trying to kill everyone?" She shook her head. "It was a whole ordeal."

"Was it hard to go back to school?" I asked.

"Yeah, a little bit," Violet said. "We all had to go in groups to talk to the counselor and everything. And all the teachers kept promising us over and over again that the school was safe and that the world is a good place and that there are just sometimes people in it who do bad things."

Counselors. Just like Uncle Toby said. It didn't make a lot of sense, though. Violet seemed, well, she wasn't exactly normal. But she was talking. She was out. She seemed just fine.

So why wasn't TJ?

It just didn't add up.

There was a low roll of thunder from somewhere in the distance. "Oh," Violet said, sitting up a little in her lawn chair. "I *hate it* when the weather forecast lies. There was only supposed to be a five percent chance of rain today. I don't have time for this noise."

I shrugged. "Sorry?" I said. I didn't know why I felt the need to apologize. It wasn't my fault that Violet was disappointed in the weather.

"How's TJ doing, anyway?" She asked it so suddenly that it nearly gave me whiplash.

"What?" I said.

"TJ. Your cousin. Remember? How's he doing? I know it hasn't been easy for him. He never comes out to play in the water." She gestured to the kids with the inflatable pool. "And he did that all the time, last summer. I was holding dibs then, too."

"He's...uh." What could I say? "I don't know. He's... well. He's really, really quiet."

He isn't talking.

But I couldn't bring myself to say it.

"So, not so great?"

"No."

37

She nodded. "Is he still sneaking out?"

"Is he still *what*?"

In my head, I heard the sound of a needle scratching a record. A sound effect the internet loved to pair with shocking information.

Violet couldn't be serious.

Sneaking out?

"Sneeeeeeakiiiiing"—she spoke slowly and loudly—"ooooooout."

"What are you talking about?" I asked.

"I've seen him," she said. "Sometimes at night. Usually after dinnertime. He comes out." She pointed to the front door of the apartment building. "And heads off that way." Her fingers walked the sidewalk, down to the far end of the block.

"Where does he go?" I asked.

"I don't know," Violet said. "I just know it's sneaky."

"How do you know?"

"Well, he's not allowed outside after dinner by himself."

"How do you know *that*?"

"I make it my business to know what's happening in the neighborhood," she said smugly. Leaning over in her chair, she pointed to the girl bouncing the soccer ball off her head. "Daisy Jackson isn't allowed to date until she's sixteen, so she has to meet her boyfriend at the corner any time they want to go out together." She pointed at one of

38

the little kids in the pool, a girl with an enormous head of black curls, slipping and sliding on the grass. "Deanna Merchant is allergic to peanuts and strawberries, so she's not allowed to eat dinner at anyone's house." She pointed to another kid, this one a thin, blond boy with hair like the head of a dandelion. "Perry Michaelson got after-school detention three days in a row when he told Ms. Lipski that she was stupid." She turned back to me. "And those are TJ's mother's rules. No going outside alone after dinner."

"Oh." I frowned, brushing one of my fake curls back, behind my ear. "That's...I don't know what that is," I admitted. "It's weird. Him sneaking out. So weird."

Violet looked up at me. There was a hunger in her eyes. She wanted to know what I knew. "Isn't it?"

Well, it wasn't TJ. I knew that. My little cousin didn't go out by himself. Except for the fact that he apparently did.

So what was my responsibility here?

Was it my job to tell Uncle Toby and Aunt Lisa?

Probably.

But how could I tell them when I didn't know what there *was* to tell?

You couldn't share a story until you knew it.

So that's what I would do.

Learn the story.

If nothing else, I was sure that it was the key to helping TJ.

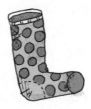

CHAPTER THREE

I hid my phone under the table.

Aunt Lisa didn't allow cell phones during dinner, but I was on a quest and I couldn't stop now.

I searched for "sneaking out." Not surprisingly, I didn't find an answer right away. Instead, I pulled up a bunch of articles in teen magazines, offering tips on the best ways to sneak out without getting caught. Apparently, TJ had already mastered that part. I scrolled down, down, down, until I stumbled on a list of popular movies about sneaking out.

I knew it had nothing to do with TJ, but I was curious, so I clicked on it.

Ten clicks later and I realized that I was reading about the history of Pixar.

So I went back to the start. New search terms: "why do kids sneak out?"

The problem was that Aunt Lisa was eyeing me like a hawk, so it was hard to read more than a few sentences at a time. She seemed to be taking some kind of weird pleasure in watching me eat. I could only search in little, stolen moments—when she got up to find the pepper or refill her glass of water or open the window.

Dinner was catfish, buttery squash, and a sugar-free pecan pie for dessert.

"I haven't made most of these dishes in years," Aunt Lisa said, resting her chin in her palm. "We've turned into a real take-out family. Glad to know I haven't completely lost my touch." Her stare was a little creepy, but I kind of got why she was watching me. I didn't see TJ take a single bite. He cut his food up into tiny pieces and pushed those pieces around on the plate, so it looked like a rodent had been nibbling away at his dinner. And no matter how much Aunt Lisa tried to get him to eat, he just sat there stubbornly, his eyes never really focusing on any one thing.

Until there was a loud boom from the street.

I guess it was a car backfiring. A sound that was half like a firecracker and half like a door slamming shut. I heard it so often in Deerwood Park that I'd sort of forgotten it was a thing. We just ignored it and life went on.

But TJ heard it.

He let out a sound—the first I'd heard him make. It was like some kind of animal. A wail that came from a place deep inside. His face wrinkled in terror. He curled in on himself and fell under the ledge of the table. Aunt Lisa let out a gasp, and Uncle Toby immediately hopped out of his seat, knocking over the bottle of orange pop he'd been hiding behind his chair leg. I leaned over to one side to get a better look, slipping my phone under my napkin. Uncle Toby pulled TJ up against his chest, hugging him tightly.

"It's all right," he said, stroking TJ's hair. "It's all right, kiddo. Just a car. Nothing to worry about."

"You're safe," Aunt Lisa said, leaning over the two of them, putting her hand on top of TJ's head. "Totally and completely safe. With your parents and your cousin who love you very much."

The fear on TJ's face dissolved as quickly as it came. But there was no relief after. He didn't take comfort in the way that Uncle Toby held him. And none of Aunt Lisa's whispering seemed to reach him. His face was like glass. Immovable.

The three of them sat like that for a good, long while—pop puddling on the floor beside them—before TJ turned to face his mom.

Aunt Lisa sighed. "It's all right," she said. "You can go to your room if you want, sweetie."

TJ stood up, robotically turning from the table and walking down the hall, disappearing into his room as the swollen floorboards creaked under his feet.

With a swish, the door closed behind him.

Uncle Toby sat on his knees, grabbing a napkin to absently mop up the pop on the floor. And the three of us just fell silent. I tried to pick at my food a little. But that felt like pretending. I couldn't pretend that whole thing hadn't happened.

Could I?

I started to ask. "What just—"

"Finish your veggies, Leah." Aunt Lisa cut me off sharply.

I finished my veggies.

The cabinet behind the table was calling to me. After dinner, as Uncle Toby sat on the couch, watching—but not really watching—a Cubs game, I heard the cabinet whisper. It was promising me answers. Stone-cold facts. I wondered if I could sneak over and find Aunt Lisa's binder, look through it for some kind of explanation of what had happened at the table. Without getting caught. I got all the way to the cabinet and even got the door open, but then I heard the sticky smacking of Aunt Lisa's bare feet approaching the living room. In a panic, I grabbed the first thing I saw, which happened to be TJ's old one-hundred-piece jigsaw puzzle of an ice cream sundae, oozing with hot fudge and strawberry sauce.

Aunt Lisa walked in just in time for me to close the cabinet and make a big show of holding up the puzzle.

She seemed to accept that.

Deflating a little, I walked back over to the carpet and lay down on my stomach. I spilled the pieces on the floor and started to turn them over, upside down so I was looking at the brown, cardboard backs. I'd put together the puzzle so many times it would be too easy any other way.

My phone vibrated, and I slipped it out of my pocket. Nicole was texting me back, finally:

Miss you too. How's your family doing?

I had no idea how to answer her. Not without getting emotional, anyway. So I put my phone away and started putting together the puzzle.

Even without the picture to help me, I still managed to finish in about five minutes.

"Show-off," Uncle Toby said, glancing over at the plain, cardboard square in front of me.

I took out my phone again and snapped a photo of it. Maybe this is what I would have to send Nicole tomorrow morning. It seemed to summarize my summer perfectly. A big, blank stretch of nothing. And it would be a way around answering her question.

As I started to break down the puzzle again, I heard a sound. At first, I thought it was a Cubs fan screaming thinly from the stadium seats on TV. Certainly, that's what Uncle Toby seemed to think, because he didn't stir an inch. But I knew that sound.

It wasn't a baseball fan.

It was a floorboard.

I picked up my phone and started tapping the screen with my thumbs, pretending I was sending a text. But the screen was blank, a smooth black surface, a dark mirror that showed me what was happening over my shoulder.

It showed me a tiny, nearly eight-year-old boy as he crept down the hall, his footsteps almost lost beneath the sound of the crowd singing "Take Me Out to the Ball Game."

TJ was wearing jeans and an old, ratty T-shirt with a picture of the Chicago flag on it—four red stars between two pale blue stripes. He moved with care. He knew which boards were the noisiest and which wouldn't make a sound. Expert precision. In a way, it looked like he was dancing, skirting from one side of the hall to the other. When he hit the living room, he dropped down to all fours, sliding along the bottom of the wall, just beneath the height of the couch, so Uncle Toby couldn't see him.

When he got to the front door, I wondered what he would do. There was no way to open it without being seen. He waited. And waited. And waited some more. I was absolutely sure that he was stuck. Until I heard Aunt Lisa over by the table, going over her project materials.

"Toby," she called.

"Yes, *bubbeleh*?" Uncle Toby said, glancing over his shoulder toward the table. I cringed at his nauseating pet name for her. It was the Yiddish equivalent of "baby cakes" or "sugar lumps" or something like that, and the last thing I wanted to hear was them getting all lovey-dovey.

But them getting mushy was all that TJ needed. The second his dad's back was turned, he bolted, grabbing the door and opening it just enough to slip out. He rotated the handle before he closed it again, so the bolt didn't make a sound as it slid back into place.

It was so fast, I would have missed it, if I'd looked away from my screen.

"Can I get your opinion on something?" Aunt Lisa continued, missing the whole thing.

"Sure," Uncle Toby said.

"Hey," I said, sitting up on my heels. "Would it be all right if I went outside for a little bit?"

"Of course," Aunt Lisa said.

At the exact same time, Uncle Toby said, "No."

There was a moment of silence, before she came padding over to the couch, her hands firmly planted on her hips. "Toby..."

"It's not safe, *bubbeleh*," Uncle Toby said.

"It's Oak Lake," she said. "No place safer on Earth."

"Not after Chancelor—"

"We can't let Chancelor dictate the rest of our lives," she said. "Or ruin how we feel in our own home."

"I'll stay between Keating and Downey," I said, getting to my feet. I was losing time. I had only seconds, I knew it.

"She'll be perfectly safe, Toby."

Uncle Toby looked back and forth between the two of us but seemed to know he was outnumbered. "Oh, all right," he said. "But be back as soon as the streetlights come on. And take your phone with you."

Aunt Lisa laughed. "I don't think that's going to be a problem. Leah's addicted to that thing."

"Am not," I said, but already I was shoving it into my back pocket as I rushed for the door.

"Don't forget, the code to get back in is—"

"One-seven-zero-one," I said. "I know!"

I heard Aunt Lisa tsking and muttering behind me, but I didn't look back.

I took the cement stairs two at a time, racing as fast as I could.

TJ couldn't have gotten far.

Could he?

Outside, it was a warm and humid evening. So humid that I immediately felt a sheen of sweat on my face. In the distance, thunder rolled.

Violet's weather forecast was super wrong.

It was going to pour.

But I turned my back on the storm and hurried along the sidewalk. I remembered the direction Violet had pointed when she told me about how TJ was sneaking around, so that's the way I went. It was only a block or so before I spotted him.

He was walking differently. Around the apartment, he moved like a zombie, shuffling his feet, looking anywhere but forward. Now he moved with purpose. There was a lightness to his step. I wouldn't call it skipping or anything like that. But it wasn't a shuffle, that was for sure.

Nothing so heavy.

For a second, I thought about calling out to him.

Maybe he would tell me where he was going.

Maybe he would share his secret.

But maybe he wouldn't.

No, I decided. Better not to let him know I was there. Not yet, anyway.

Better to see how he acted when he thought he was alone. Maybe *that* was my first step to helping him.

Or maybe I was just completely lost and making up the rules as I went.

TJ was so far beyond the limits set by Keating and Downey that I guess he sort of figured he was safe. That no one was going to come after him. He didn't look back, didn't check over his shoulder. He just kept walking down the sidewalk, uninterested in the gathering storm.

We made our way past bumper-to-bumper cars, crammed together so tightly against the curb that it was no wonder Violet guarded her dad's space the way she did. Rows and rows of town houses. Beautiful, green trees, shivering their leaves in the wind. But then, suddenly, we rounded a corner and we were in the city.

Not Chicago proper. No skyscrapers or freeways or giant metal beans.

Not the kind of city you saw in pictures and in the opening credits for the nightly news.

The quieter city. Softer.

A milder version.

I heard the train rumbling overhead on a high, metal track. Sparks crackled and died beneath its wheels, in the shadows of the station. The streets suddenly had stoplights. Crosswalks. Awnings. They were lined with small shops rather than homes. There were more than just kids out, hanging around. Grown-ups—wearing steely gray and blue suits, carrying briefcases and messenger bags—passed without really noticing one another, walking in a chaotic jumble that somehow managed to avoid collision. It was only a few blocks, but it felt like another world completely.

One that Uncle Toby didn't think was safe.

But not TJ.

He didn't show any fear.

He just kept walking.

Good for him. Being afraid was a waste of energy. Like crying.

I was suddenly so proud of my tough, little cousin.

I continued to follow, at least half a block behind. With all the people racing to and from the train station, I had to bob and weave between them in order to keep my eyes on TJ. He was so small that the crowd threatened to swallow him up.

He passed under the wide tracks, rounding a few rows of bike racks, mostly empty now. When he started to turn, I pressed myself against the side of the stairwell, leading up to the train platform. Between the spokes of the railing, I could just see him, if I stood up on my tiptoes. He moved through the bike racks and into the dark shadows against the wall of the station.

"Hey, little man," a gruff, unfamiliar voice said.

"Hey, Morgan!"

For a second, time seemed to stop.

That was TJ. My cousin still had his voice after all. He spoke! I felt a ridiculous rush of excitement and had to clamp my hands over my mouth to keep from yowling. *Control yourself, Leah.* But all the same, it was such a victory.

He *spoke*.

He spoke!

But who was this Morgan?

How had he broken the spell? I knew it was completely unfair, but all of a sudden, I felt kind of jealous. I was supposed to be the one who managed to get through to TJ. I had all kinds of plans and suddenly...it was someone else.

Someone clearly more special than I was.

Carefully, I edged my way around the stairs and under the tracks, squatting down behind a bike that looked like it had been locked on the rack for years. The metal on the frame was orange and rusted. The tires flat, completely deflated. And there was a spider that had made itself a lovely web between the handlebars. Spiderwebs were supposed to have healing properties. I'd read that on Wikipedia. And it seemed to be true, as I watched my cousin transform through the silken threads of the web.

Sitting on a plastic milk crate, in front of the little doughnut shop built under the tracks of the train station, there was a man who I could only assume was Morgan. I couldn't tell how old he was, exactly, but he seemed kind of ancient. The top of his head was bald and splotched, but there was long, stringy white hair running in a rim around it. It hung over the canvas band of a visor, featuring a glittering, pink doughnut with blue and purple sprinkles. Under his apron with a matching logo, he was wearing a shirt that had probably once been white. Now it was yellowed with age, sagging under his armpits.

"You going to bring me something good today?" Morgan asked, looking up at TJ with a wide grin. One of his front teeth was cracked and jagged.

"Hope so," TJ said, raising one shoulder all the way up to his ear.

"Good," Morgan said. "I can't wait."

Across the street, someone slammed a car door.

TJ yelped, dropping down to the pavement at Morgan's feet, curling his head to his knees.

"Hey, hey," Morgan said, touching TJ's back gingerly with the tips of his crooked fingers. "Just a car, little man. Just a car."

I wanted to rush over and drop down beside him, holding him in my arms like Uncle Toby.

But TJ surprised me.

He sat up, all on his own. Swallowing hard. He was still kind of scared, but better now. Getting less and less afraid by the second. What a tough, little guy.

He could control it!

He could control it?

But what was ... *it*?

"Don't worry," Morgan said. "I get that way some-times, too. Loud noises are the worst, aren't they?"

"Yeah," TJ said, shrugging his shoulder again. Slowly, he pulled himself up to his feet, smoothing down the front of his shirt. "I'll see you later, Morgan, okay?"

"See you later, little man. Might even be a doughnut in it for you." He winked.

"Thanks!"

Morgan held up his hand. He was wearing a plastic glove. Without hesitating, TJ gave him a high five before he turned and ran back around the bike racks, continuing down the sidewalk.

What in the world?

I stood up quickly and stumbled after him, throwing a swift look over at Morgan. He was smiling, shaking his head a little bit as he stood, slipping two fingers through the handle of his milk crate and swinging it back behind the register in front of the display of doughnuts.

A man wearing a Chicago Bulls jersey stopped beside the little shop, chatting on his phone as he examined a menu board with prices.

"What can I get for you?" Morgan asked, peeling off his glove.

No time for questions.

Even if there were a million of them.

TJ was half a block ahead of me when he stopped. I pulled myself behind an enormous plastic recycling bin, crouching down. TJ opened the door to a storefront and slipped inside, letting it slam shut behind him.

I looked up at the sign:

Squeaky Green Coin-Op Laundromat

Why would TJ go there?

His apartment building had a washer and dryer in the basement.

And TJ certainly didn't do laundry.

Slowly, I came out around the recycling bin and moved closer to the door. It was made of glass, so I could see inside. There were rows of washing machines running across the Formica floor. And on the far side, the entire wall was made of dryers stacked on top of dryers. A couple of people were going about their business inside. A woman my mom's age, sitting on top of a machine, flipping through a magazine. Two guys who looked like underwear models, standing beside one of the dryers, arguing about something. And a lady with hair teased up to roughly the size of a house, daintily separating her light clothes from her dark clothes on a small table in the corner, her fingertips ending in enormous red talons.

I didn't see TJ.

Should I go inside?

I don't know why I hesitated. I guess because I knew I wasn't supposed to be there. And it was more than just breaking Aunt Lisa's rules. TJ had gone there thinking he was alone. How would he feel if he saw me?

Would he ever speak again?

To me?

To anyone?

Two steps to the door. Three back. Another step forward. Two steps back.

I couldn't make up my mind!

Which, I guess, meant it had to be made up for me.

A crack of thunder, louder than before, echoed across the sky. And suddenly the heavens opened up.

Fat, heavy drops started to fall, pelting my head and shoulders.

All around me, the people coming and going dug into their bags and briefcases, pulling out umbrellas that snapped open to the tune of a beating drum.

I grabbed a newspaper from the recycling bin and held it up over my head, using it as my own umbrella, but I was already drenched, my fake blond curls stuck against the sides of my face.

I had to get back to Uncle Toby and Aunt Lisa's. They thought I was only down the block. If I didn't come running inside after a few moments in the rain, they'd start to suspect I went beyond Keating and Downey.

And if they suspected me, they might suspect TJ, too.

I couldn't do that to him.

Before I took off, though, I grabbed my phone. It slipped in my wet hands, but I managed to get it unlocked, and I took a picture of the sign over the coin-op.

For research purposes.

Doing my best to shield my head from the rain, I started to run, hurrying back to the safety of Oak Lake's town houses and trees. All around me, people were rushing this way and that. The only stillness I could see was Morgan, leaning against the countertop of his little doughnut shop under the train tracks, watching the rain fall with a distant sort of look in his eyes.

I wondered what he was looking at.

The same thing TJ looked at when he was staring off into space?

Maybe.

But I didn't bother trying to figure it out. I was too excited by my new discovery:

He was *talking*.

CHAPTER FOUR

"Have you ever heard of Squeaky Green Coin-Op?"

I had to wait more than twelve hours before I was able to ask.

Twelve hours that nearly drove me bonkers!

Although I left the laundromat and buzzed myself back into the apartment without so much as a single question, I found that a part of me was still lingering on that sidewalk, staring through the glass door, looking for TJ. What was he doing there? What did that place give him? Why did he speak to Morgan, when he wasn't talking to his own family? Was there someone else he was talking to? Would he ever speak to me or any of us again? And what could *I* do in all of this?

The questions continued whispering in my ear all night long, the unfinished story keeping me wide awake. The kind of awake that made you angry at your pillow.

Not that I was ready to let myself get angry.

In the morning, I noticed that TJ had slipped back inside without being caught. I wondered what time he'd gotten back in. Probably sometime after he knew Uncle Toby and Aunt Lisa would leave the living room, but before they would check on him in bed. Smart kid. He sat at the breakfast table, moving his scrambled eggs around on his plate, without actually eating a bite.

His voice seemed like a distant memory.

Had I dreamed it?

I didn't think so.

Fortunately, I knew exactly who to ask for information about anything in the neighborhood.

Violet raised both of her eyebrows at my question. She was sitting in her lawn chair, her long legs stretched out in front of her, crossed at the ankles. She'd been working on another list—apparently, a list of all the materials she'd need for her high school applications, even though it was still a year until she had to start applying. But when I asked, she paused. "Squeaky Green Coin-Op?" she said. "Yeah, I know it. The place down on Frank Street, right? Between the hot dog stand and the shoe store."

"Yeah."

"It's been there for decades." She shrugged. "What about it?"

"I don't know, you tell me," I said, sitting on the curb. Aside from two stray Yelp reviews, Squeaky Green didn't have a web presence at all, which was *so* annoying. I'd searched and searched for hours, until it was three in the morning and I was watching a YouTube video of Kermit the Frog singing "Bein' Green." Decidedly off the map, I'd given up on finding Squeaky Green's digital footprint. But I wasn't sure what I'd look for on their website anyway, even if I found one. There probably wasn't a page called "Reasons why your cousin might sneak in." The internet wasn't *that* friendly. Fortunately, I had Violet.

"What do you know about it?"

"It's owned by Livia Green," Violet said. "Been in the Green family for years. Livia's got three kids. One in high school, one in middle school, and the youngest is about TJ's age. All of them went to Chancelor, at one point or another. Two boys and a girl. Their father left Chicago about five years ago. Military. I don't think he and Livia ever got married. Right now, Livia is dating a guy who works at the—"

I knew I'd come to the right person.

"But what about the laundromat?" I asked, leaning forward.

"I don't know," Violet said, turning back to her list. "It's a laundromat."

"Anything interesting about it?"

"What could be interesting about a laundromat?" Violet asked.

"I don't know," I said. "That's what I'm trying to figure out."

She sighed. "What are you talking about, Leah?"

I hesitated. It wasn't so much that Violet was the biggest know-it-all gossip I'd ever met. I wasn't worried about her ratting me out to Aunt Lisa. I just knew I needed to decide if it was worth breaking TJ's trust. Trust that didn't really belong to me in the first place. Honestly, I didn't know what to do. But if I was ever going to reach TJ, I knew I had to do *something*. Violet could be a big help.

After a moment, I let out a sigh and nodded, my mind made up. This was for TJ. "My cousin snuck in there last night."

Violet dropped her pen. "What?"

I had a feeling that it wasn't often someone beat Violet to a juicy piece of information like that. Leaning over, I picked up the pen and handed it to her. "TJ snuck into the laundromat."

"How do you know?" she asked.

"Because I followed him."

"Leah Abramowitz," she said, pronouncing my name perfectly, "there's a devious streak in you." She gave me a full-braces grin. "I like it."

I stared at her for a second. I certainly didn't think of myself as devious. But all right. "Uh...thanks?"

"Tell, tell!"

"There isn't enough to tell, really," I said. "I followed him there and saw him go in. That's it. I was hoping you could fill in the details for me. Is there anything you know? Anything that could explain—"

"No," Violet said, shaking her head. "Absolutely nothing."

"I was afraid of that."

"Sneaking to the hot dog place, I could get. Sneaking to the shoe shop—if TJ really liked shoes—I could get. But a coin-op?" She paused. "Your aunt's building has a washer and dryer, right?"

Somehow, it didn't surprise me she knew that. I just nodded. "In the basement."

"Well, that is officially weird." She swung her legs around, over the arm of the chair, so that she was facing me. With the notebook on her lap, she flipped to a fresh page and started scribbling notes. "Snuck into Squeaky Green last night," she said as she wrote. "Same direction he always goes in." She glanced up at me. "Do you think he goes there every time he sneaks out?"

I hadn't thought about that. "No clue."

"Unclear if he goes there every night." She wrote almost as quickly as she spoke. "Do you know if—"

"I don't know anything! That's why I'm asking."

Violet hooked her pen through the spiral of her notebook. "I'm just trying to collect all the facts."

"I don't have a lot of those."

"Well, seems to me that's the first step."

"What?"

"Finding out more."

I shrugged. "I guess."

"So, it's settled," she said, slapping her palms against her knees. "We follow him tonight."

"Right." I paused. "What?"

"Weeeeeeeee foooooooollooooooooow hiiiiiim tooooonight."

We?

When I looked up at Violet, she was grinning. Not a pretty grin. Not a movie-star-on-the-cover-of-a-magazine grin. More like the villain in a spy movie, plotting the destruction of Earth. You know, if villains in a spy movie wore braces and were twelve. "I figure, we have a pretty good line of sight to your front door from right here." She pointed just a little ways down the street. "All we have to do is wait. It's the easiest stakeout ever."

Easiest stakeout ever? Maybe Violet really was a supervillain. What kind of kid actually went on stakeouts? I didn't even want to ask. Anyway, I was still trying to figure out how to uninvite her. The last thing I wanted was to put TJ on display.

But Violet continued making plans. "It's usually a little after seven that he gets going." She added that note to her collection. "I'll tell you what. You call your aunt and tell her that I invited you to dinner at my place. We won't really go to my house, of course. We can just grab snacks and have a picnic in the spot. That way we'll be sure not to miss him."

"What about your dad's dibs?"

She waved her hand dismissively. "Weren't you listening? I said we'll have a picnic. Blankets. Lawn chairs. The whole thing. Dibs secure."

"But you said Chicago drivers—"

"Anyway, my father should probably get home before TJ sets out," she said, buzzing away. "We can hang out in the car. He lets me borrow the keys sometimes, as long as I don't try to drive it or anything. Honestly, it's the only place I can go to listen to my music without my sisters bothering me. Hey, that reminds me! Do you like Dina and the Starlights? I have their latest album, and it's the best thing ever."

"Violet, I'm not sure that—"

"I'm thinking of writing up a review of it for my school newspaper."

"I don't think—"

"If you don't like Dina, I guess I can forgive you for that. I mean, it's seriously wrong. But I can forgive it. I also have Electric Diamond. And the soundtrack to *Hamilton*, if that's your kind of thing."

"Could you just—"

"Of course, *Hamilton* is everyone's thing, I think," she continued. "I mean, it's got a little bit of everything and it—"

"Violet!"

She blinked, staring at me with those shockingly blue eyes of hers. "What?" she said.

I took a deep breath. "It's really nice of you to want to help me, Violet," I said. "But I don't know that it's a good idea."

"Why not?"

"Because..."

"That's not a reason," she said, impatient and pouty.

"It's nothing personal, Violet. It's just that I—"

"What?"

"I..."

"You what?"

"Ugh!" I stamped both my feet in agitation and then immediately felt bad about it. I couldn't afford to get so frustrated. I swallowed it back. "I don't want you telling stories about TJ. If it's something...if it's something bad."

Violet swung her legs down, off the arm of the chair. She stood up and walked over to me. And for a second, she just stood in front of me. Towered over me. But then, she sat down. Sitting on the curb beside me, she was all sharp angles. Elbows and knees. But her voice was soft and mild. "Something bad?" she asked. "What does that mean?"

"I wish I knew." I shook my head, staring down at the way our shadows reached across the width of the parking space. "There's something wrong with my cousin, Violet. And I want to help him, but I don't know how. It...it's bothering me. A lot."

I regretted saying it.

That was the kind of thing I kept to myself. Maybe I told Nicole, if it was really bad. But mostly myself.

"Well, of course it's bothering you." She knocked her shoulder against mine. "I mean, there'd be something very wrong with you if you weren't worried about your cousin."

Her answer caught me off guard. There were plenty of queen bees in my school. The kids who knew everything about everyone. Who collected gossip, hoarding it, waiting for just the right moment to use it.

To sting.

They didn't say things like that.

They didn't act like they cared.

I guess there was a flip side to knowing everything about everyone. Maybe it was entirely possible that you could know everything about everyone and actually *care* about everyone, too.

At least a little bit.

"Hey," Violet said, putting a hand on my elbow, "I'm not going to go telling stories about your cousin, okay? I just want to help."

"Really?"

She shrugged. "Either you believe me, or you don't. Doesn't matter. I'm going with you."

There were a thousand different ways to interpret what she was saying. Maybe she was just bored and needed something to do. Maybe she was nosy. Or maybe, just maybe, Violet really was interested in helping me.

I decided that was what I wanted.

So it was what I chose to believe.

CHAPTER FIVE

Aunt Lisa sent me back three smiley faces and a pink heart when I texted her that I'd made friends with another kid in the neighborhood. I had a feeling those smiley faces were Aunt Lisa's way of saying *I told you so* about making friends, but I decided not to worry about it.

She needed to be right about something. She needed a win.

As it turned out, agreeing to hang out with Violet that day ended up being one of the best decisions I ever made.

The two of us had absolutely nothing in common.

Zip.

Zero.

Zilch.

I lived alone with my mom, who was a college professor. Violet was one of four daughters to a Vietnamese mom and Polish dad—a web designer and a science teacher, respectively. I liked putting together puzzles and drones. She liked to write and make lists. I knew every single word to every single song by Selena Gomez. She made a face at the mention of Selena Gomez, calling her music "basic" and insisting that Dina and the Starlights were much, much better.

With so many differences, I figured that we'd never run out of things to say.

And I was right.

We talked and talked the whole afternoon.

"I don't see any words," she said, when I showed her the word fortune predictor I'd sent Nicole.

"You just have to let your eyes relax," I told her.

Violet scrunched up her face. Kind of the opposite of relaxing, really. But after a moment, her expression brightened. "Oh!"

"See something?"

"Yeah."

"What?"

"I see 'big.' "

"Okay, that's a start. Keep looking."

"And…" Violet's eyes swept back and forth. "Oh! 'Neat.' "

" 'Neat'?"

"And 'star.' "

"All right," I said. " 'Big.' 'Neat.' 'Star.' I guess that means you're going to be a big star on YouTube, who teaches people how to organize their closet space." All things considered, not the worst future to imagine for her. I would have taken something like that. I followed at least three dozen different YouTube channels religiously. And I wished I could come up with one of my own, for when I was old enough to have it. Thirteen was only a year away.

But again, there was nothing special enough about me.

Channel owners all had some kind of gimmick. One was good at putting on makeup. Another was good at playing the guitar. And another could figure out what every single detail in any movie trailer meant.

I didn't have a gimmick of my own.

I just seemed to obsess over the gimmicks of others.

Violet chuckled. "How do you come up with a future like that?"

I shrugged. "I don't know."

"Hey, what do you want to be when you grow up?"

I stared at her a moment. "You know, you think about the future a lot. Has anyone ever told you that?"

She waved her hand. Unapologetic. "The future will be here before you know it. You have to plan ahead." She gave me a nudge with her fingertips. "So?"

"So what?"

"So what do you want to be? When you grow up?"

"I...don't know," I admitted. "I don't think about the future all that much."

"Why not?"

"Because you never know what it'll be like. Your life can change in a snap." I snapped my fingers. "One minute, you're one thing; the next minute, you're something else."

Like, one minute, you were living in a house with two happy parents. The next, you were in an apartment and your dad didn't want anything to do with you, because he was too busy living a happy life on the other side of the country with his replacement family. His two stepsons— my stepbrothers—loved *Star Wars*.

I hated it.

"That doesn't mean you can't imagine," Violet said.

"When you don't know what the future's going to be, you're just guessing."

"Everyone guesses."

"I don't." I much preferred facts.

Violet looked skeptical. "Oh," she said.

"Honestly, I'm not sure what I want to do when I grow up," I said. "I just know that I want to be..."

"What?"

"Don't laugh."

"I won't. Unless it's really, really funny."

I glared at her. But after a moment, I let out a sigh and said, "Special."

"Special?"

"Yeah."

"What does that mean?"

"I don't really know yet. I just want to find something that... that I'm really good at. Something that no one else can do the way I do it."

"Okay, what do you like to do?"

"Well..."

"Yeeeeeees?"

I ducked my head, feeling a little sheepish. I'd never told anyone this before. "I sometimes like to read Wikipedia pages. For fun."

Violet stared at me for a moment with her computer-blue eyes, not even blinking. It definitely wasn't a normal use of the internet. And we both knew it. "What kind of pages?" she asked.

I shrugged. "All kinds. Anything that seems interesting."

She raised both eyebrows. "Not so sure how useful that is."

"It can be useful, sometimes."

"How?"

"I once read the Wikipedia page about Twinkies. Did you know that the original filling flavor for Twinkies was banana?"

"I can't say that I did," Violet said. "But seriously, I'm not sure how knowing about Twinkies is all that useful."

"Well, I'm on my school's quiz bowl team."

"What's quiz bowl?"

Ha ha. Finally something Violet *didn't* know everything about. "Trivia competitions. Just answering questions. Anyway, this one time, the question was about the original flavor of Twinkies. And I knew it."

Violet shook her head a little bit. "All right. So knowing about Twinkies is *sometimes* useful. Although I don't think you can be a professional quiz bowler."

"Probably not," I said. Although I had heard about people who made small fortunes as champions on game shows.

"What else do you like?"

I thought about it for a moment. "Stories." I'd never told anyone that before, either. Not that it was an embarrassing secret or anything. I guess it was just strange. I held up my phone with the word fortune predictor. "I like putting together stories."

"So you could write—"

"Not writing, exactly," I said. "Not making things up. Not pretending. More like putting together the pieces. Like a jigsaw puzzle."

"I'm not sure I get it."

"I don't, either," I said. I couldn't find the right word

for it, let alone a way to turn it into some kind of future. So I shrugged and changed the topic a little. "Maybe I could be a photographer. I take pictures all the time."

"Well, that's perfect," Violet said, brightening.

"Perfect?"

"Maybe we'll work together when we're older. I'll need a photographer."

"So you already know what you're going to be when you grow up?" Can't say I was all that surprised, given Violet's obsession with the future.

Violet nodded. "I've known ever since I was six years old."

"What?"

"I'm going to be a journalist."

"You want to write—"

"Not write," she said. "*Report*. There's a huge difference."

"What do you mean?"

"Writers create stories," she said. "Reporters report stories. You don't make it up. You tell it like it is."

I could see what she meant. "Where are you going to get the stories?" I asked.

She shrugged. "I don't know. Other people. I mean, every person has some kind of story, right?"

"I guess so."

"They all need to be told. I think the stories will find me."

"You don't care what it is?"

"Not really."

"But what if you don't like the story?"

"It doesn't matter if I like it," she replied. "A story is a story. It exists in the world, which means it needs to be told."

"You think so?"

"That's just the way it is."

"Okay." Who was I to argue?

"Now," Violet said. "I think you should take my picture."

She struck a very, very serious pose.

It involved winking one eye and sticking out her tongue.

Around dinnertime, while I held her dad's dibs, Violet ran into her house for snacks. I checked my phone and found a text from Nicole:

> **You're not answering. What's up? That's not like you.**

She knew me a little bit too well sometimes.

I sent back the quickest reply I could think of:

> **Things are weird.**

That would have to do. Honest, but not too emotional.

I'd find a way to explain it to her later. When I knew what to explain.

Violet returned, her arms filled with granola bars, bananas, juice boxes, and bags of cookies. We spread out a plastic tarp and then put down a blanket and ate in the spot, using her lawn chair as a table between us. The blanket was a beautiful patchwork quilt that Violet's mom had sewn out of old dresses and shirts.

"This," she said, pointing to a silvery blue square, made of fake velvet, "was the dress I wore to last year's Winter Wonderland Dance. My sister spilled grape juice on it two months later. We couldn't get the stain out, so it got donated to the quilt. And this"—she pointed to a patch of peachy pink—"is from a bridesmaid dress my mother wore when she was in college. I saw a picture of it. One sleeve. Kind of looked like a shower curtain. Very, very ugly."

"What about this one?" I asked, pointing to a square of liquidy gold.

"My sister's Halloween costume from three years ago. I think she was supposed to be a Greek goddess or something, but she was so shiny that, really, she just looked like a baked potato wrapped in foil. Not the best-quality fabric, but as long as I'm careful when I wash it, it shouldn't dissolve."

The block flowed around us as we sat there. Kids came out and ran around. We watched the working crowd return home. I took pictures of the shadows as they swept around the pavement, changing directions. When Violet's dad drove up, we cleared away the picnic so he could slide his car into the spot, parallel to the curb. Then he gave Violet the key, to let us sit in the car with the windows open.

"Now it's a real stakeout," Violet said, pointing out the windshield, to the front door to Uncle Toby and Aunt Lisa's building.

"Yeah," I agreed.

Except for the part where we were sitting in the back seat. In the movies, the undercover cops usually sat in the front.

Also, I was pretty sure that undercover cops didn't listen to Dina and the Starlights. But Violet was so excited to play their latest single for me:

> *Some people walk with giants*
> *Others look like demigods*
> *Some laugh into the lightning*
> *Me, I felt like a fraud*
>
> *Couldn't find the way*
> *To get my life off the ground*
> *But you can't really lose*
> *What was meant to be found*

A little after seven, we saw the door to Uncle Toby and Aunt Lisa's apartment building open. We both sat up, leaning forward with our chins pressed against the front seat headrests. And there he was. TJ. Walking down the front stairs and turning right, in the direction of Squeaky Green.

"This is it," Violet said, reaching her long, spindly arm between the seats to turn off the music.

"Yeah," I said.

We slipped out of the car, closing the windows. And once Violet locked it up and tucked her notebook under her arm, we started hurrying along the sidewalk, jumping over puddles and out of the way of several dog walkers.

I was going to get some answers tonight. I was determined.

And then I would use them to help TJ.

And then TJ was going to talk to everyone again.

Things would go back to normal.

CHAPTER SIX

It helped that TJ was following the exact same path as the night before. It made it easier for us to stay far back, to move at a leisurely pace. I only wished Violet hadn't worn flip-flops. True to their name, they flipped and flopped with every step she took. The noise was so loud I couldn't believe that TJ didn't hear it. But he wasn't the one trying to be sneaky. He was completely carefree, his arms swinging at his sides.

He was holding something. It was in his left hand, his fingers curled so tight around it that I couldn't tell what it was.

Just that it was something red.

We followed him around the corner and out into the

business part of the neighborhood. A train had just rolled into the station, and there was a chime as the doors slid open. Dozens of people got off, but even more seemed to get on. With another chime, the doors slid closed. I was amazed that they were able to shut, with all the people jammed inside. But somehow, they managed.

When TJ drifted under the train tracks, I held out an arm to stop Violet.

Together, we slipped up against the steps to the train platform, looking behind the bike racks.

"Hey, little man," Morgan said, giving TJ his big, wide grin. He was in the same matching hat and apron as the day before, but this time, instead of an off-white shirt, he was wearing a shirt that probably used to be blue but had faded to gray.

"Hi, Morgan."

That sweet voice again. It hadn't been a dream.

He was talking.

I felt Violet squeeze my shoulder. I reached back to grab her arm. I wasn't gripping her arm because I was feeling emotional, or anything like that. I just needed to keep her from talking.

"Bring something for me today?" Morgan asked. He was just peeling off a pair of plastic gloves. With all the people swarming around the station, he didn't have any customers. I guess it was too late in the day for doughnuts.

"Yup," TJ said. He uncurled his fingers, revealing a bright red bottle cap.

A bottle cap?

I was pretty sure that's what it was. I'd managed to accidentally stumble on Uncle Toby's secret supply of orange pop. It really wasn't so secret. He'd just stashed the bottles in one of the drawers of his desk in the study. They were lined up like little soldiers, with gleaming red caps, stamped with logos.

Morgan took the bottle cap with a little chuckle. "You can never go wrong with something sleek and red, in bottle caps or cars." And he let the bottle cap tumble over his knuckles, his fingers rippling.

"Why is your cousin handing out trash?" Violet hissed in my ear.

I shook my head slightly.

"Thanks, little man," Morgan said, slipping it into the big front pocket of his apron. "This guy is a classic."

"Glad you like it," TJ said.

"Got anything else for me?"

"Um, I'm not sure yet," he replied. "I have to go check first."

"Go check?" Violet said. "Go check what?"

It was a very good question. An amazingly reporterish question, I was sure. But I didn't know why she was asking me.

I didn't know.

Morgan chuckled. "That's okay, little man."

"I'll see you later, Morgan," TJ said.

"See you later."

TJ smiled and waved his hand and went back to the sidewalk, passing through to the other side of the tracks, on his way to Squeaky Green. I assumed, anyway. Morgan watched him go. And his shoulders seemed to deflate a little bit when TJ was gone. With a sigh, he reached behind the counter and pulled out his milk crate, sitting down heavily in front of the shop.

No customers.

Violet looked at me. "Well. That was strange." She sat in silent deliberation for a moment. And then she nodded. "Let's find out more."

"Find out more?"

"Yes. Fiiiiiiiind ooooooooooout mooooooooooore."

With that, she walked under the bridge.

And I realized what she was doing.

"Violet!" I said. "Wait!"

But Violet didn't wait. She walked through the bike racks, dodging a couple of guys who'd just claimed their bikes. With her head up and her shoulders back, she made her way over to Morgan.

I let out a soft groan.

What was she *thinking*?

"Hi," Violet said, looking down at Morgan.

He looked up at her, a small smile playing across his lips. "Hello, hello. What can I do for you this evening?" He started to stand up. "Did you want some doughnuts?"

"No, no." Violet shook her head and Morgan sat down again. She took out her notebook, flipping to the page with all her notes about TJ. "Who was that little boy you were just talking to?"

"Violet!" I hissed, crossing under the tracks. I lingered by the bike racks. Morgan seemed harmless, but apparently, I was the only one who payed attention to the lessons we were taught in school about talking to strangers. Especially grown-ups.

"Oh, relax," Violet said, barely even glancing my way. "It's just Morgan."

"What?"

"Everyone knows Morgan." Violet waved her hand dismissively, as she continued her interview. "The little boy," she said. "How do you know him?"

"Little man?" Morgan asked. "Oh, he comes around here for a visit every day, about this time."

She scribbled a note. "He does?"

"Sure. Sure." He wiped his hands down over the curve of his knees.

"Does he always talk to you?" she asked.

"Most nights. Usually brings me something, too."
He was talking.

"Brings you something?" She paused, the tip of her pen touching the paper, leaving a smear of ink.

"Bottle caps."

"Bottle caps?"

"I collect them," Morgan said, taking the one TJ had just given him out of his pocket to show her.

Violet wrinkled up her nose. "Oh."

Morgan looked over at me, squinting his tired, deep-set eyes. "You look just like him. Are you little man's sister?" he asked.

"Cousin," I said, shrinking back half a step.

He chuckled. "You don't have to be shy, Cousin. I won't bite."

He said "I won't," not "I don't."

I tried to laugh. It didn't sound terribly convincing.

"Morgan! Morgan!"

It happened too fast for me to stop it.

TJ came racing back under the bridge from out of nowhere, waving a fist in the air like he was carrying the Olympic torch. He was running straight for Morgan. But then he saw Violet. And then he saw me.

In some ways, it felt like the first time he'd seen me— really, really seen me—since I'd arrived. It wasn't with his glossy-eyed, colorless stare, tucked in the shadows of his bedroom. He was alert. Awake. Alive. And we both knew it.

The surprise only lasted a second.

And then the anger replaced it.

"What are *you* doing here?" he asked me.

"TJ." I couldn't breathe. I couldn't think. This so wasn't how I'd wanted our stakeout to go. It was all wrong. So wrong.

"You *followed* me?" he said.

I didn't know what to say.

But, naturally, Violet did.

"Of course we followed you," she said, planting her hand on her hip. "Your cousin's been worried about you."

"Yeah," I said, my voice cracking.

TJ glared at us, first Violet, then me. "You shouldn't be following me, Leah," he said.

"Hey, little man," Morgan said. He'd slipped the bottle cap back in his pocket and was shaking his head, arms folded across his chest. "Don't be hard on your cousin."

The reminder that Morgan was there seemed to soften TJ's temper. A little bit, anyway.

"Here," he said, brushing past Violet to go to Morgan. "I brought this for you." He was holding another bottle cap. This one was green and yellow. I saw a logo on top but couldn't read it.

Morgan laughed and wheezed, almost at the same time. "Hey," he said. "Thanks, little man. You're a pal."

"So are you two friends, then?" Violet asked, looking between them.

"You know me," Morgan said. "I'm friends with everyone."

"But how long has TJ been bringing you bottle caps?" she asked, writing again.

"Oh, a little while."

Violet's pen paused, and she looked over at me. I knew we were both wondering the same thing: *Why?*

Morgan took the bottle cap from TJ, his hands shivering a little bit as he dropped it in his pocket. "Don't you be upset," he said to TJ. "It's not nice to be upset with ladies. It's bad luck."

"She's not a lady," TJ said, shrugging one shoulder up against his ear. "She's my cousin."

"And what am I?" Violet asked.

"Nosy," I said, trying to make a joke out of the whole thing. I didn't like the way TJ was glaring at me.

Violet snorted.

TJ did not.

"You going to Squeaky's place?" Morgan asked.

TJ tucked one foot behind the other, shifting his weight back and forth a little bit. "Well, I was," he said, nipping at his lower lip.

"You go on," Morgan said. "And you take these fine young ladies with you."

The suggestion made TJ gasp, ready to argue that there was no way he was going to bring us along.

"You heard the man," Violet said, before he could say anything. "We're fine young ladies. You should take us to Squeaky's."

TJ looked at me. "Are you going to tell on me?"

I held up my hands. "Hey, if I get you in trouble, I get myself in trouble," I said. "I'm not supposed to be out here, either, Hedgehog."

He gave that a moment's consideration. And then nodded. It was true. We were basically locked into each other's secrets now, whether he liked it or not. Obviously, he didn't like it. But he accepted it. Because after a moment, he sighed, his shoulder deflating a little bit. "All right," he said. "You can come with me."

"Great!" Violet said, clapping her hands together.

TJ looked like he really, really didn't want to bring Violet along. But Violet wasn't going to give him the chance to argue.

She flashed a big smile before nodding to Morgan. "Thanks, Morgan," she said.

Morgan smiled at her. "Thank *you*."

Violet walked over to me, looping her arm around mine. "Let's see what there is to see at Squeaky Green."

"Fine," TJ said. "But you better be nice."

I looked at Violet, wondering if she understood what he meant by that. But Violet just looked back at me. The same question was written on her face.

Nice to who?

I supposed we would just have to find out together.

With TJ leading the way, we left Morgan behind and walked out from under the train tracks, down the block, heading to Squeaky Green.

CHAPTER SEVEN

There was a little bell that jingled when the door opened. It rang again when the door swung shut behind us. It was my first time in a coin-op and, almost immediately, I loved everything about it. There was a warm, lingering scent in the air. Fresh laundry and clean sheets. Soap and mountain rain. It was amazing. Like being wrapped up in a blanket, or my mom's arms when she was wearing a new sweater. Safe and loved and content.

I remembered once reading on Wikipedia that the sense of smell was connected to your emotional memory.

For the first time, I realized it was true.

So many happy memories.

I thought of our old house and lazy Sunday mornings and the days when my dad would—

Well. This wasn't about me.

If TJ had told me right then and there that the smell—and the way it made him feel—was the only reason he was spending so much time in Squeaky Green, I probably would have believed him.

At least, for the moment.

Even Violet, who never really seemed to run out of things to say, paused for a second as we crossed over the threshold, raising her chin and breathing it in. "Mmm," she buzzed on the exhale.

There were three back-to-back rows of washing machines across the middle of the room. Most of them were empty, their lids yawning open, waiting to be filled. The few that were running rumbled in place, laundry spinning in the little windows on front, like portholes of a shipwrecked vessel.

The wall of dryers across the back of the coin-op were stacked two high. The doors were all shut, creating a white, glossy surface. Like a sheet of ice. There were a few benches in front of the dryers, where customers were sitting. Chatting on their phones. Scrolling across the screens of tablets. Doing crosswords in the newspaper. None of them seemed that interested in us. Not at first.

But when one woman looked up and saw us standing there, she grinned and waved. "Hey, TJ," she said.

Several more looked up from what they were doing. A chorus of greetings descended upon us.

"Hi, TJ."

"How's it going, TJ?"

"Good to see you, TJ."

Why was it strangers seemed to know my cousin better than I did?

Not that it bothered me or anything.

Well. Maybe it did. A little bit.

TJ smiled and waved back at them as a group, but he crossed the room, straight to the back left corner.

Violet and I exchanged a look and followed him.

There was a door tucked away, between the edge of the wall of dryers and the washing machine in the last row. The sign in front read STAFF ONLY, but that didn't stop TJ. He knocked. And then turned to look at me and Violet.

"You better be nice," he muttered again.

A warning.

"You said that before. Nice to *who*?" Violet asked.

It seemed like a reasonable question.

But TJ didn't answer.

"Niiiiiiiiiiiiice toooo whooo?" she asked again.

On the other side of the door, there was a quick knocking pattern—three quick knocks, two more, and then three again. When it finished, TJ repeated the pattern on his side. The knocker on the other side gave a second, more complicated pattern—four knocks, one, five knocks, and then two. TJ repeated it flawlessly.

Violet glanced over her shoulder at me.

I shrugged. "Secret code?"

The door swung open.

TJ disappeared inside. Violet and I ran to catch up with him before the door closed on us.

I don't know what we were expecting, but I wasn't expecting anything quite so...normal.

The room behind the dryers was nothing more than a little white kitchen. Counters ran along the left-hand and back walls, with cabinets of white plastic. There was a beat-up, old table against the right-hand wall, with four mismatched chairs around it. One was a metal folding chair. One was black plastic, with little square-shaped holes in the back of the seat. One was a squashy chair with a pattern of flowers, like you might find in a living room. The final chair was wooden, with a cracked leather seat. Piled high on the table was laundry. Stacks and stacks of laundry. In every color imaginable.

Standing on one foot, beside the table, was a girl.

If you just let your eyes graze over her, there was nothing all that different about her. It was only if you were paying attention that you realized she was...

Well.

She was special.

It was like she was a shining light of special. It radiated out of her. Everything I kind of wanted to be but couldn't be.

She was shorter than Violet, but taller than me. Her skin was a smooth, dark brown, and she had eyes like marbles. Pure black. So dark you could see your reflection in them. She wore her dark hair in what looked like hundreds, maybe thousands of little braids, thinner than my littlest finger. There were shocks of gold woven into the braids. At first I thought they were beads, but when I looked again, I saw I was wrong. They weren't beads. They were keys. Threaded along her braids were dozens of keys, all of them a dull, gold-colored metal, with jagged edges and diamond-shaped tops. When the girl pivoted—balancing on one foot—to look at me and Violet, the keys in her hair jangled, making her sound like some kind of human wind chime. What was it like for her to hear that every time she moved?

I couldn't imagine.

She wore a long button-down shirt. The kind the men in my mom's office wore. Except this one was stained pink, unevenly, sometimes light and sometimes dark. Like someone left a wet red sock on top of it, in a pile of laundry. The sleeves had been cut off, but roughly, so there were loose threads falling down her arms. Her jeans were normal enough, at first glance. But on second glance, I noticed there were stickers all over them. Wrinkled, faded stickers. Some of superheroes. Some enchanted creatures. And some of them the sort of stickers that you found on a banana peel.

"You brought friends," the girl said to TJ. Her voice was surprisingly high. She had to be at least twelve, but she sounded like a little kid. "That's lovely. It's always so nice to have friends."

"Not really," TJ said. He made a vague gesture in my direction. "This is my cousin Leah."

That one stung a little.

I swallowed it.

"A pleasure to make your acquaintance," the girl said. She set her foot down and reached out, offering me her hand. I noticed that she was wearing a ring on each finger. They weren't fancy rings of gold or silver. Certainly, there were no precious stones on them. Actually, they looked like they were made out of plastic. They had spiders and neon shamrocks and footballs on them. The sort of rings that you might find decorating cupcakes from the grocery store.

"Hi," I said.

She continued to hold her hand out, staring at me without blinking, filled with expectation. I felt Violet give me a nudge. She was probably feeling a little triumphant right about now. She was big on handshakes, after all.

Frowning, I took the girl's hand, giving it a shake.

Firm, like Violet said.

But not too firm.

The rings clacked against each other when she shook back.

TJ gestured to Violet. "And this is—"

"Violet Kowalski," the girl said, raising her foot again, bent at the knee. She went up on her tiptoes on the other foot so that she was nearly Violet's height.

Violet tilted her head. "I know you," she said. "You're in my grade. You're Michelle Green, right?"

The girl—Michelle—smiled. "Yes, indeed. Michelle Olivia Green." Out of nowhere, she put on a fancy English accent. Like someone in a movie about elves and dragon slaying. "Of the Oak Lake Greens, of course. Charmed, I'm sure."

Violet smiled slightly. "Of course."

"Violet's my neighbor," TJ said flatly.

"How wonderful. Well, I'm glad you're here," Michelle said, going back to her normal voice.

"You are?" TJ asked, looking the slightest bit betrayed.

"I love surprises," she said. "They're little gifts that you get to keep for a second or two." She sounded so dreamy when she said it.

"Uh, sure?" Violet said.

94

Michelle turned to TJ. "Did you give Morgan the bottle cap?"

"Uh-huh," he said.

"Great. Why don't you go eat a protein bar?" she said, nodding to a box of them on the counter to one side. Her hair jingled brightly. "Then we can get to work."

"Wait." Violet whipped out her notebook. "Work?"

"Put that away," TJ said, batting at Violet's notebook. "You're not a feelings doctor."

A feelings doctor?

Like a counselor?

I remembered Ms. Weinstein. And how Uncle Toby said that TJ didn't like her.

"Put the notebook away, Violet," I said softly.

Violet sighed. "Oh, *fine*," she said. And she slipped her pen into the spiral of her notebook, setting it down on the floor, holding both hands up like she was surrendering.

The second it was out of her hands, TJ walked over to the box of protein bars on the counter and pulled one out. Right before our eyes, he ripped the top of the wrapper off with his teeth and then took a big bite.

A strange sense of relief flooded my chest.

He *was* eating something after all.

Well, of course, he *had* to be. He'd be in the hospital by now if he wasn't eating anything. But it was such a relief to see it with my own eyes.

"That works out well," Michelle said to Violet. "You going hands-free. I could use a couple extra sets of hands tonight, as it happens."

"What do you have?" TJ asked, swallowing loudly.

She nodded to the pile of laundry on the table. "My absolute, all-time favorites, of course: socks."

I looked over and that's when I realized it: The stacks and stacks of laundry piled up on the table were all socks. Every single piece. Socks with little pink hearts. Socks with stripes. Socks with moose antlers sewn along either side. Socks with holes in the toes. Socks with holes in the heels.

Socks.

Socks.

Socks.

I had never seen so many in my life. I wanted to reach into my pocket for my phone, to take a picture of them.

"Wow," TJ said, popping the rest of the protein bar into his mouth and walking over to the table. "That's a really great haul."

I noticed that his eyes were different. In the apartment, they were drained and lifeless. But looking at the pile of socks, they took on a silvery sheen.

TJ used to look at me with those eyes.

"Every one I've found over the last week or two," Michelle said. "Shall we play a game?"

96

TJ nodded. "Yes, yes!"

"Wait," Violet said. "A game? What game?"

"The greatest game in the whole universe. The sock game," Michelle said.

"Match-the-sock," TJ said.

Violet raised both eyebrows.

"These are all the socks that get left behind in the dryers," Michelle explained, setting her foot down and drifting over to the pile. She moved like an exotic bird, a flamingo or something. But with the lightest of treads. "I used to play this game with my little brother all the time. The game is to see if any of them are matching."

"And if they are?" Violet asked.

"Then we donate them to the YWCA."

"And if they aren't?"

Michelle leaned over, raising her jeans at the knees. She wasn't wearing shoes! On her left foot, she was wearing a neon pink sock with white bands around the toe and heel, a pattern of gold birds crisscrossing the sides. On her right foot, she had a pale blue sock with purple dots of different sizes.

"Well," Violet said. "That's quite the fashion statement."

"Thank you very much," Michelle said, dipping into a curtsy. I don't think I'd ever seen anyone curtsy before. Not in real life. That was what they did in the past, wasn't it? I remembered from movies. When lords and ladies greeted royalty, they curtsied just like Michelle.

It was the kind of thing you only did if you were wearing the cone-shaped hat Nicole was wearing at camp.

Weird.

"Michelle is the best at finding things," TJ said.

I looked over at him, but he was happily elbow-deep in a pile of socks, pulling one after another out, holding them together to see how they looked.

He seemed so different.

So, well, the same. The same as the little boy I remembered from back before March. The boy who had clumsy fingers but tried his hardest to fit together pieces of the same puzzle every time. The boy who smiled. The boy who begged me to read picture books with him. Who wowed me with the stories he wrote as part of his hundred words a day. The little hedgehog with twitchy ears. Who practically cooed when you gave him a hug. The cousin in all my photos from last year.

The boy who'd vanished.

I'd wanted to find him and bring him back.

I'd found him.

But I hadn't done anything to bring him back.

Michelle had.

Somehow.

"What sort of things does she find?" I asked, unable to take my eyes off him. What sort of things, other than my long-lost cousin, that was.

"All kinds of things," TJ said.

"That's specific," Violet droned.

TJ looked up at Michelle. "Show her."

Michelle shrugged. "Well, you can see the pile-o-socks for yourself," she said, gesturing to the table.

"But there's so much more," TJ said.

"True." Michelle skipped over to a counter on the other side of the room. There was a large mason jar filled with loose coins. "This is all the change that people leave behind in the washers and dryers," she said. "We really aren't a coin-op anymore. Not really. You don't put coins in the machine. You just add cash to a plastic card and use that to do your laundry. The coins are all just…leftovers."

"What do you do with them?" Violet asked. I could see her eyes cut over to her notebook, longing for it.

"Anything I want," Michelle replied. "Finders keepers. Sometimes, we give it to charity. Sometimes, I use it to accessorize."

"Accessorize?"

Michelle slipped her thumb through one of the many necklaces around her neck. They were all on cloth strings. The one she lifted was a piece of black twine, threaded through a purple plastic charm shaped like a top hat. There were others, in every possible color. A bird. A lily pad. A ballet slipper. A soccer ball. A fried egg. "I get them from the gumball machines at the hot dog place next door."

"And the keys?" Violet continued, gesturing to Michelle's hair.

"They get caught in the machines. No one ever comes to claim them. Guess they don't realize they've lost them. Or it's just easier to get new keys. Or they're never going back to wherever they came from."

"I told you," TJ said, balling up a pair of nearly matching blue socks. "Michelle is the best at finding things."

Michelle walked to the line of cabinets along the back of the room. She opened all the doors, slipping her pinky finger through the white handles. I'd been expecting to see the same sort of junk as at my mom's office: coffee cups, pads of paper, pens and pencils, staplers, those bear-shaped bottles of honey. Instead, the cabinets were full of shoeboxes.

"Shoes?" Violet asked, sounding hopeful.

"Better than that," TJ said.

Michelle struck a pose, like a model on an old game show, pulling back a sequined curtain to reveal a brand-new car. Except, instead of a car, she pulled out one of the boxes and took off the lid. There was an explosion of color inside. Curled like snakes, there were dozens and dozens of ribbons, most of them with fraying edges.

"Okay, then," Violet said, her forehead crinkling.

Glad to know we were both confused.

The next box Michelle took out was filled with key

chains. They came in every possible shape, advertising every possible place, from the Ferris wheel at Navy Pier to the hot dog place next door to the renaissance fair my social studies class visited for a field trip, just over the border in Wisconsin.

Each box was filled with similar treasures.

Candy-bar wrappers.

Single mittens.

Broken necklace chains.

Buttons.

Left-behind things.

Lost things.

Honestly, things that I wouldn't have even noticed were missing, for the most part.

But TJ, oh, TJ was just amazed by the collection. He grinned at each box, as the top came off. He oohed and aahed at Michelle's entire collection.

"Come on," Michelle said, as she put away the shoebox filled with paper clips. "Help us match up socks."

It wasn't really my idea of fun, but when Violet looked at me, I just shrugged and headed over to the table. She followed me. And the four of us started pulling out socks, trying to match them together.

On the other side of the door, someone slammed the lid on a machine. It was as abrupt and as uncomfortable a sound as the car backfiring the night before, but when I looked over at TJ, my heart jumping into my throat, he just barely flinched his shoulders. I would almost have guessed he didn't hear the sound at all.

No wailing.

No hiding under the table.

That had been a completely different person.

"What do you think, Michelle?" TJ asked after a few minutes, holding up two brown socks.

"I think that no one should ever wear brown socks," Violet said.

"Close," Michelle said. "But that one on the left is a little bit darker, you see? Hold it in the light, buddy."

TJ frowned at them for a moment, shifting slightly to the left, under the fluorescent light. And then nodded. "I guess you're right," he said. And he dropped the darker one back on the pile, still on the hunt for a match for the lighter sock.

None of it made any sense.

It was less than that.

It was completely senseless.

But there was my cousin. Out of his shell and happily talking with Michelle about socks, of all things. He was so completely determined to find the missing sock. All of his focus and energy was on the piles.

And after a while, he found it.

Or something near enough.

"Good job!" Michelle said.

TJ beamed as he folded the matching socks together and set them aside.

"Sooooo," Violet said. I noticed that her fingers twitched, like she was trying to reach for her pen again but stopped herself. "Michelle. TJ. How do you two know each other?"

"We met outside of the land of feelings," Michelle said. "The building that scrapes the sky and overlooks the water."

A moment of silence passed. Violet caught my eye, before turning back to Michelle. "Meaning?"

"Ms. Weinstein's office," she said. "It's in the Plaza 550 building, by the lake. I was at the vending machine. My little brother was in the 'feelings room' with my mama. That's what they call the little room with the blue couch, which I think is a much better name than 'the little room with the blue couch.' My brother didn't want me to go in with him. He thinks he's too old to hang out with his big sister now. So I was getting a snack. And I was lonely, until I found TJ."

"*Found* him?" Violet said.

"He was lost."

"Or he ran away," I said, remembering what Uncle Toby told me.

TJ ducked his head, looking a little embarrassed.

"I think I was meant to find him," Michelle said.

"Meant to?" Violet said.

Michelle shrugged. "I like being a big sister. And if my brother is too old for me now, I guess fate decided to send me a new little brother to take care of."

I thought maybe Michelle was joking. But she didn't laugh.

If anything, she seemed even more serene than before.

It wasn't fair. If such a thing as fate existed—and I wasn't sure it did—shouldn't it have been *my* fate to take care of TJ?

What was it about Michelle that brought him back to us? Finding lost things? Socks and keys and quarters?

No.

No, I refused to believe it.

There had to be something more about her. Something that made her special. Something she possessed that...

Well. Something that I didn't have. That Uncle Toby didn't have. And Aunt Lisa. And anyone else.

I tried not to be jealous, but it was hard.

Maybe it was my job to figure out what made Michelle special. If I found it, maybe I could duplicate it. I could do it myself. Teach Uncle Toby and Aunt Lisa. I just had to discover what it was, give it a name. Which meant I was going to be spending a lot more time at Squeaky Green.

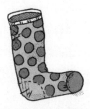

CHAPTER EIGHT

I expected to get the full rundown about Michelle Green the next morning, when I met up with Violet in her dad's parking spot. What clubs she belonged to. Who she was friends with. Her teachers. Her grades. Her shoe size. Even the number of bugs that she'd swallowed as a kid. I don't know. All of the details that Violet so carefully collected about everyone else in that busy, buzzy brain of hers.

But she surprised me.

"There's nothing to tell," she said, as she carefully made a couple of notes in her notebook. She was working on her holiday gift list.

You know, in July.

"Nothing to tell?" I felt like the road map had just been snatched out of my hands, leaving me lost again.

Violet shrugged. "Not really. No one really knows much of anything about Michelle Green," she said. "She sort of keeps to herself. Her older brother, Willy, is a superstar basketball player at a high school on the North Side. And her little brother, Jamal, is freakishly smart. He's already in middle school math. He sheltered in place with my class during the..." She trailed off a moment, before she shook her head and cleared her throat. "But Michelle is just kind of lost in the middle, I guess. I don't know, really."

"Clubs?"

"No clubs. Not that I know of, anyway. Which is really going to be a problem when she applies to high school. They look for that kind of thing on your application."

"Were you ever in class together?"

"Not that I can remember. But you have to understand, Chancelor is a very, very big school."

I narrowed my eyes. "A girl goes around school wearing keys in her hair and there aren't any stories about her? Nothing at all? Really?"

"Oh, the keys are new," Violet said. "There's no way I wouldn't have noticed that." She paused. "And I kind of like them."

Violet's lack of gossip was disappointing. But fine. I could figure out things for myself. Find my own way. And now that TJ knew he'd been followed, he agreed to go to Squeaky Green in the afternoon, with us, instead of leading us along at night. As long as we didn't tell his parents.

"Promise me, Leah," he said. "*Promise* me."

I agreed.

Although I didn't promise not to tell Nicole. So I did, in a long, thirteen-part text late that very night, when it should have been lights-out time in her cabin.

She replied anyway:

You'll figure it out, Leah. You always do.

I was grateful for her confidence in me.

She knew me. She knew the harder the puzzle, the more I wanted to dig in.

And it was an upside-down puzzle, all right. With more than one hundred easy pieces.

Anyway, Uncle Toby looked about ready to burst into tears when I told him that I was going on a walk *with TJ*.

"That's wonderful!" he said, pulling me into a strangling hug.

"Uncle Toby!" He was hot and sweaty.

He grabbed my face and planted kisses all over it.

"Ew! Stop slobbering on me!"

"Slobbering? This is nothing! Have I ever told you about the time I found a saber-toothed tiger frozen in a block of ice? We thawed her out and kept her as a pet at the CIA headquarters for a few weeks. Now, that girl really knew how to slobber. She was always licking my face, like..." He turned up his chin and started to lick the air with his tongue.

"Let's go, TJ," I said, putting a hand on his shoulder and steering him out the door before it could get any grosser.

We helped Violet pile all the lawn furniture she could find in her parents' storage locker into her dad's parking space. And then the three of us walked down the same old path, back to Squeaky Green.

TJ made Violet leave her notebook behind.

The table had a big box on it, with the words "Lost and Found" written on one side, in permanent marker. After letting us in the back room, Michelle—who was wearing a long, pink sundress with mismatched socks, one peachy orange, one black with white polka dots—climbed up on top of the table and perched down beside it. "Hear ye, hear ye!" she cried, using her dragon-slaying movie accent, "gather ye around and see what there is to see!"

"What are you *doing*?" Violet said.

She went back to her normal voice again. "Just playing."

"Playing?"

"Don't you ever play?"

"I *report*," Violet said.

"Oh. I'm so sorry." Michelle actually looked very sad.

"What do we have today?" TJ asked, pointing to the box.

Michelle's sadness melted away. "All this stuff has been here over three months," she said, taking out a necklace strung with purple glass beads.

"Pretty!" I said.

"We have to go through it and decide what we can and can't keep."

"What can't you keep?" Violet asked.

"Things people might miss," Michelle said. She rattled the necklace, the beads clinking. "Like this."

Violet nodded, looking thoughtful. "Well, then. We should come up with a plan of attack."

TJ looked at her. "What kind of attack?"

"Not a real attack," Michelle said. "She means a—"

"A system," Violet said.

"I have an idea," I said, walking over to peer inside the box. "We should sort through the box and divide everything into groups." I took a quick peek at the things jumbled together. "Clothing. Jewelry. *Broken* jewelry. Buttons. Ribbons. Keys. Socks—I know they're clothing, but they're a special kind of clothing, I think." There were just so many of them. "Office supplies. Pens. And miscellany."

Both of Violet's eyebrows went up. She looked impressed. "You came up with all those categories after looking at the box for two seconds?"

I shrugged. "Yes?"

Had I really managed to impress her? Didn't seem like a big deal to me. Nothing special. All you had to do was look and see.

"What's miscellany?" TJ asked.

"Stuff that doesn't fit into the other categories," I said, trying to hide a little amazement. I never got to teach TJ new words! "The really, *really* lost stuff. We'll figure out what to do with that pile last." I paused, looking over at Michelle. "If that's okay with you." It seemed reasonable to ask. This was Michelle's territory, after all.

But Michelle nodded. "That sounds perfect. I've never tried having a plan before. It'll be fun!"

"Okay!" TJ said, planting his hands on the table. He tried to jump up and hoist himself on top, but didn't quite have the lift for it. Michelle grabbed him by the wrists and gave a pull. For a moment, his legs dangled over the ground, peddling like he was on a bike, but then he managed to hitch his knee up on the table and pull himself over the edge. At once, he threw himself halfway into the box, his butt pointed straight up, wiggling as he started digging through the things.

Violet chuckled. "What are you doing there, TJ?"

"Looking all the way to the bottom!" he said.

"Meanwhile, we're just looking at a bottom," Violet said.

Michelle let out an abrupt squeal of laughter that seemed to come from nowhere and disappear as quickly as it arrived.

TJ jerked his head up and looked at her for a second, frozen. I guess her squeal was just a little too sudden. But he saw it was just Michelle and went back to digging.

Good boy, I thought. *Keeping himself calm.*

I still didn't know what to make of the scene at dinner, with the car backfiring. But so far, he hadn't repeated it. Not with Michelle around, anyway.

We started to divide the lost and found into piles, the categories that I came up with. I was surprised by the sheer amount of stuff that had been lost and left behind. Some of it, like the purple necklace, was really cool. We found a silky scarf, white with purple and black flowers printed across it. A loose button, shaped like a daisy with a pink stone in the middle of the petals. And two CTA cards.

Other things were just disgusting. We found a nearly empty notebook, its pages crinkled by a dried coffee stain along the bottom edge, which TJ slid as far away from Violet as possible. A pocket-sized teddy bear, half of its fur washed off. A Styrofoam cup filled with sunflower seed shells. And a smooth white stone, which was either a broken piece of a button or a tooth. We couldn't tell for sure.

We decided not to look too closely. Because. *Ew.*

Those went in the miscellany pile. Although Violet suggested they immediately go into the trash instead.

Michelle, Violet, and I didn't have much to say. We worked carefully, trying not to gag at some of the grosser stuff.

It was TJ who did most of the talking.

"And then, after we finished at the Coca-Cola museum, we went to the aquarium and saw a whole lot of fishes. Then we went to this really, really big building that's also a studio and it's where a news channel called CNN lives."

He was talking about a trip to Atlanta he took with Uncle Toby and Aunt Lisa, about a year ago.

He was talking.

Violet looked up sharply. "You went on a tour of CNN?" she asked. And she definitely sounded kind of jealous.

"Yeah," he said, shrugging one shoulder. "And after we visited CNN, we went to a restaurant that was a tearoom that Mommy said was famous. And I had something called cheese grits, which was really, really good."

"Sounds like all you did on that trip was eat, buddy," Michelle said. "If I ever went on a vacation, I'd want to do more than that."

"If?" Violet said. "You don't go on vacations?"

"Well, not real ones," Michelle replied. "We don't really have enough money. We have to pay for Willy's basketball

112

equipment and Jamal's therapy. But I do like to go on vacations in my head."

"What?"

"Sometimes I close my eyes and I go for a quick trip to ancient Greece." To demonstrate, she closed her eyes, her long eyelashes jet-black and shining in the light.

Violet just stared at her.

"It's really quite lovely this time of year. The water of the Mediterranean Sea is a perfect blue, and the sea nymphs are out all day, sunning themselves on the rocks." She opened her eyes and turned back to TJ. "But keep going about Atlanta. Besides the food, I mean. So far, you've told me about the peach cobbler, the fried chicken, the dumplings, the Coca-Cola, and now the cheese grits."

He'd also, I noticed, gone through three of Michelle's protein bars.

"Mommy says that the best part of growing up in Atlanta was the food, but she *also* says Chicago food is better, especially the pizza."

"What do you think?"

"I think Mommy's right," TJ said. "Chicago food is better. I really, really like our pizza."

"Me too," Michelle said.

"Me three," I added.

"Who doesn't like pizza?" Violet asked.

TJ was talking about pizza. It was such a little thing.

But it suddenly felt bigger, coming from him. I was replaying every word he said, again and again, trying to figure out what it all meant. But it didn't seem to mean anything. He was just talking.

About anything.

This, that, and the other thing.

Mostly food.

Like a normal kid.

And Michelle wasn't doing anything special to get it out of him. Well, she listened, I guess. I remembered the brief glimpse I'd gotten of Aunt Lisa's lists. At the top of all of them was "Listen to your child." But there was nothing supersecret or hidden about the way Michelle listened. Nothing I could figure out on my own.

I didn't get it.

Once we'd sorted the whole lost-and-found box, I had us further divide things up. Michelle had a shoebox for every possible find. Beads. Erasers. Lip balms. Business cards, some of them so thoroughly washed that you couldn't really read the print anymore.

A place for everything.

We put it all away, and I was amazed by how exhausted I felt.

Lost things were surprisingly hard work.

We sat down in the mismatched chairs around the table to take a break. There were still the socks to deal with, but our tired feet needed a rest. "Jamal used to always help me with the socks," Michelle murmured, looking wistful, as if she were staring into a past she missed terribly.

I remembered the name. Michelle's little brother. The one who was apparently freakishly smart, according to Violet. The one in middle school math, even though he was TJ's age.

The one in therapy.

"Where is he?" Violet asked, glancing from side to side, as if she expected him to appear suddenly.

"He doesn't come to Squeaky Green anymore," Michelle said. She sighed heavily. "Says all our games are just kid stuff."

"Kid stuff?"

"Yeah. He's too big for it all now and doesn't need them and doesn't need me."

"Ouch."

Michelle looked over at Violet, her lips parting just slightly. "Thank you," she said.

Violet blinked. "Huh?"

"For saying that."

"What?"

"It does...hurt."

"Oh." Violet squirmed a little bit. "I'm sorry, I guess."

"Where's Jamal now?" I asked.

Michelle shrugged. "He just spends all his time locked in his room, playing games on his computer."

Violet snorted. "And *that's* not kid stuff?"

"I don't know." Michelle was silent for a moment. More than a moment. And when she started speaking again, it was more like she was talking to herself. "He thinks that being a big kid is what saved his..."

His what? I leaned forward, waiting for Michelle to finish the thought, but she shook her head.

"Do either of you have brothers?" she asked, like she'd suddenly realized we were in the room with her.

"No," Violet said.

I shook my head. No brothers. Just *step*brothers. And I never saw them, anyway.

I had TJ, of course. At least, he used to be like a brother.

Sweetly, he reached over to put a hand on Michelle's shoulder. Like he was trying to comfort her. She looked down at him and smiled.

She was holding a long yellow-and-black-striped sock by the toes, running it between her fingers. The fabric kept getting caught on the sharp corner of one of her rings, one shaped like a hockey stick. For a moment, she looked at it thoughtfully, tilting her head from side to side, before she suddenly stood up and walked over to Violet. "Put this on your hand," she said, holding out the sock.

Violet looked up, both eyebrows shooting to her hairline. "Excuse me?"

"I have an idea."

"What kind of an idea?"

"Just trust me! It'll be fun! Jamal and I used to do this all the time!"

I could tell Violet wasn't too sure about Michelle's idea of fun. Neither was I. But after a moment, she sighed.

"Okay," she said. And Violet slipped the sock on her arm like it was a fancy evening glove.

"What are you doing?" I asked.

Michelle didn't answer. But she pressed the bend between Violet's thumb and fingers, forcing some of the sock fabric inside. Gently, she folded Violet's fingers together. She'd turned the sock into a little puppet with a mouth. "It's a bee," she said. "A magical bee from a far-away land."

TJ looked over at Violet, intrigued.

I expected Violet to snort. I could see what Jamal meant about kid stuff. And he *was* a kid. If anyone was going to complain about that sort of thing, it would be Violet. But she surprised me. She sort of smiled. And opened and closed the sock's mouth a few times. "Bzzzz," she said, moving her arm from side to side, the bee hovering in midair. "Bzzzz. My name is…" She faltered. "What's my name?"

"Queenie!" TJ said.

"Queenie." Violet raised her voice into a high-pitched squeak, opening and closing her hand to make the sock talk. "I'm the queen of the bees. Bzzzz."

I started to roll my eyes, but TJ's laughter stopped me.

He sat up in his chair—the wooden one with the cracked seat—tucking his heels under his butt, leaning forward across the table so he could watch Violet fly her hand around.

Violet turned her hand to TJ. She opened the mouth wide, letting out a gasp. "What's this? Is this a human boy?"

"Yeah," TJ said.

"Bzzzz, don't hurt me, giant human boy," Violet said.

"I'm not a giant," TJ said.

"You are to me!"

"You're the biggest bee I ever saw."

"Really? Well, that's very kind of you, giant human boy." She tilted her hand just slightly, and it gave the impression that her bee was tossing back invisible curls, like she was admiring herself in front of a mirror.

I laughed. Violet was cut out to be a queen bee.

Michelle, though, pursed her lips to one side, looking thoughtful. "A bee needs eyes to see the giant human boy," she muttered.

"What?" I said.

But Michelle was already off and running. She crossed over to the box of buttons and started sifting through them. They clattered as the box shook, like a giant maraca. She pulled two black buttons out of the mix, one a round, flat button with four holes in the middle, the other smaller and diamond-shaped, with two holes and a squiggle of thread still caught in between. She opened a drawer and grabbed a bottle of glue, bringing it all back to the table.

"Hold still," Michelle said, not to Violet but to Violet's hand. "I'm an expert. Jamal always put me in charge of the eyes. They're the most important part, you know. The eyes tell you everything."

"What was he in charge of?" I asked.

"Coming up with good names."

Violet held Queenie perfectly still as Michelle dabbed glue over her knuckles and pressed the buttons into place. "Ahh," Violet said in the Queenie voice. "That's much better. I can see so clearly now. Thank you, giant human girl."

Michelle giggled, and the keys in her hair chimed.

"Yes," Violet continued, reaching Queenie closer to TJ. "Yes, I can see, you aren't such a giant human boy after all. But you are a human boy. I hope we can *beeeeee* friends. I know that we bees have such a terrible reputation. But I promise, I won't sting you at all."

Michelle clucked her tongue. "No. Something's still missing."

"What?" Violet asked, in her regular voice.

"A queen bee needs a crown!" Michelle clapped her hands together. "That's it! All the kings and queens in olden times had them. It was all the rage!"

Boxes flew, and soon Michelle had scissors and tape. The one box I thought was most useless, the one filled with candy-bar wrappers, produced the beginnings of a crown. When Michelle turned a wrapper inside out, it was a sheet of solid, silver paper. She cut a jagged line of teeth across one edge, then looped it together and taped it in place, on top of Queenie's head.

"Oh yes, very good, very good," Violet said in the Queenie voice.

"But, of course," Michelle said, "there's something a queen needs even more than a crown."

"What's that?" TJ asked.

"A loyal knight, willing to serve her."

"Why a knight?"

"What else? Part soldier, part jock," she said. "In the old days, they were the greatest heroes of them all. Every king and queen wanted one."

"I could be that," TJ said.

"A human boy, in my court?" Violet snorted. "Certainly not."

"How about another animal?" Michelle asked, eyeing the pile of socks.

"I suppose that would be okay."

It just came out. I couldn't stop myself. "A hedgehog?" I said.

"Oh! Yes!" Violet made Queenie's mouth open wide. "Yes. A hedgehog. I'd like that very much!"

Michelle pulled a plain white sock out of the pile. "Hold out your arm, buddy," she said to TJ. He obeyed at once, letting her slip the sock over his hand.

"I'm pretty sure that's not what a hedgehog looks like," Violet said, in her normal voice.

But I was already three steps ahead of her. Phone out, I pulled up the Wikipedia page on hedgehogs and turned the screen so they could see the picture at the top.

"Oh, he's so cute!" Michelle said.

He really was.

"Needs quills," Violet said, looking at the sock on TJ's hand.

"I've got just the thing," Michelle replied. Another box came out of the cabinets. It was labeled "Pens." "Help me, Violet."

The two of them started to take pens out of the box. Carefully, they forced the little tab that people use to hang pens off their shirt pockets through the fabric of TJ's white sock. They laid them out in layers, starting low on his hand and working up higher and higher. Before our eyes, a sock became a hedgehog with pen quills in a variety of colors and sizes. They overlapped one another, making his hand look rounder.

I scanned the Wikipedia page while they worked. "Did you know that hedgehogs are nocturnal?" I said.

"What's nocturnal?" Michelle asked.

"It means they mostly sleep during the day," TJ said. "And they're most awake at night."

"Exactly!" I said. Kind of like TJ himself, who had been sleepwalking through the days and only showing a spark of life at night, inside Squeaky Green.

Once Michelle and Violet were finished with the quills, Michelle fished out two blue buttons, one big and one sort of small, and glued them over TJ's knuckles, giving the hedgehog eyes. "There we go," she said. "A hedgehog to serve the queen."

TJ worked his puppet's mouth open and closed. The pens shivered and clacked against one another, but they stayed in place, more or less. "What's his name?" he asked, looking up at Michelle.

"Well, don't ask me. You have to take a look at him. What's he look like?" Michelle said.

TJ examined the lines of pens a moment, then nodded slightly. "I think his name is Staples."

"Staples the hedgehog it is," Violet said.

"He's *Sir* Staples," Michelle said.

"Even better!"

"Hurray!" TJ said, making his reedy little voice squeak even higher than before. He bounced his hand up and down and started to open and close the hedgehog's mouth in time to his words. "I'm your loyal knight, Queen Queenie," he said to Violet's hand.

"Oh, good," Violet replied.

TJ went back to his regular voice. "But a queen needs people to rule over, doesn't she?" he asked Michelle.

"You're absolutely right!" Michelle grabbed a pink sock that was long and clingy, like it was supposed to go all the way up to the knee. Shucking off her plastic rings, she slipped it over her hand and halfway up her arm. "Find me two white buttons," she said to me.

I went over to the box and shifted through the supply. I wasn't quite sure what she was going for, but I picked out two as close to the same size as possible, big and round, each with four holes. Following her directions, I glued them to the sock, not so much on top, like the others, but on the sides. Michelle shaped the mouth with her fingers.

As I worked, I snuck a peek at TJ out of the corner of my eye. He was practicing making the hedgehog's mouth move, silently forming words and trying to re-create the shape of them with his fingers. A line formed between his eyes as he concentrated, but it wasn't a bad sort of look. He was extremely focused.

At least until Violet had Queenie exclaim, "Sir Staples! What a rude thing to say in front of your queen!"

TJ let out a peal of laughter.

"There we go," Michelle said, once her puppet had eyes. She dug into a box of markers and pulled out a black one, shading in the tips of its lips.

"And who is this new member of our court?" Violet asked in Queenie's voice.

Michelle turned the puppet to look at Queenie. And it suddenly came alive. "Huzzah and good morrow to you, my queen," Michelle said, using another over-the-top English accent. "I be-eth your loyal flamingo servant."

And yes. Somehow, it was a flamingo. The sock seemed to transform. I could see it.

"What's your name?" Queenie asked.

Michelle turned to TJ. "What do think, buddy? What's a good flamingo name?"

TJ scrunched up his face thoughtfully a moment, then nodded. "Francis," he said. "That's a good flamingo name."

"And what role do you serve in my court?" Violet asked.

"Why, the royal hairdresser, of course!" Francis turned to look at Staples. "And my goodness! Not a moment too soon! Sir Staples, your hair is looking very stiff. You need conditioner, right away!"

"No baths!" Staples cried.

Violet snorted. Michelle giggled.

And TJ?

TJ just looked so happy that he'd been able to make them laugh. He looked proud of himself.

"Hedgehogs never take baths!" he said. "We roll around in the dirt and the mud and that's how we get clean!"

"You clean with mud?" Francis asked.

"It's magical mud," Staples replied.

"Ooooooh, I see."

"Well, I don't see," Queenie said. "Francis! I demand, by royal decree, that you give my loyal knight a bath! I won't have him stinking up the palace!"

"Yes, my lady," Francis said. "Happy to serve you in all manner of matters related to filthy hair!"

"You'll have to catch me first!" cried Staples.

TJ got up and started to race to the far corner of the room. Michelle chased after him—careful to always let him stay two steps ahead of her—waving Francis about wildly and shouting out nonsense. "Fiddlesticks and puddle ducks!" she cried. "Tea and crumpets, you fiend!"

"We will have order!" Queenie said. "I demand order! This is a royal court, not a circus!"

"Oh, but, Your Majesty," Francis replied. "Don't forget you have elephants in the kitchen, preparing a great feast. And the lions and tigers will be dancing in the ballroom until all hours of the night!"

"I guess it *is* a circus!" Queenie said.

"Leah needs someone, too!" TJ said, running over to

me. He grabbed my hand and pulled me over to the table, where he started searching the socks. "What kind of animal should she be?"

"Nah." I smiled, leaning over to kiss him on the side of the head.

"Ew!" he said, wiping it off with one hand.

"I'm fine," I said. "I have my favorite Hedgehog right here." I threw my arm around his shoulders, pulling him up against my side. I didn't need to play make-believe games.

I guess it was kind of an excuse, though. I didn't think I would make a very good puppeteer. And I couldn't think of an animal that I'd want to be, anyway.

I just knew I needed to be around.

I could only wonder... what *was* my role here?

If I was going to hang around, I needed to find a purpose.

CHAPTER NINE

We left Squeaky Green when it was time for dinner. Me, TJ, and Violet. But we left Queenie and Staples behind, so they could have a sleepover with Francis, Michelle said. She didn't want him to get lonely, without his friends.

"There's nothing worse than being lonely," she said.

I didn't think twice about it, at first. If Aunt Lisa found out that the puppets were made out of castoffs from a laundromat, she would absolutely refuse to let them into her nice and clean apartment.

But leaving them behind had an effect I didn't anticipate. The farther away TJ walked from Staples, the quieter he got. He walked between me and Violet, but he didn't look up; he let us talk over his head. And when Violet asked him a question, the most she got was a nod or a grunt or a shrug of one shoulder. Until we turned back onto Uncle Toby and Aunt Lisa's street.

And then he said nothing at all.

"Did you hear me, TJ?" she said. "I asked if you knew Jamal."

Nothing.

"Michelle's little brother?"

Silence.

I knew I wasn't imagining what the last few hours had been.

But it was like they had never happened.

TJ was right back where he started. And I could hear my mom's warning echoing through my head again:

He isn't talking.

I didn't understand. It wasn't fair.

Violet frowned at me. I could tell she was wondering the same things I was wondering but didn't really know how to say it. We'd have to talk later.

For the time being, we said goodbye in front of the apartment's main entrance, and then TJ and I walked back up the cement stairs, as I programmed Violet's number into my phone.

"We had fun today, didn't we, Hedgehog?" I asked him.

TJ just kept walking, his eyes staring straight ahead.

That evening, Uncle Toby decided to barbecue. He was out on the small balcony of the apartment, standing over the grill, when we walked in. He waved at us with his tongs through the window. "Look who's back!" I could see yet another bottle of orange pop, this time hidden behind the grill, on the far side of the balcony.

"There you two are," Aunt Lisa said. She was sitting on the couch, with a book open in her lap. She was always reading something interesting, between her projects.

I tried to get a good look at the spine of her book, but all I could see was the word "psychological."

"Where have you been?"

"Why don't you tell her what we did today, Hedgehog?" I said, looking down at TJ with a little smile.

It was as if he'd turned to stone. He stood at my side, but he wasn't really there. His eyes—the color of granite— were fixed at some point in the middle of the room, half- way between me and Aunt Lisa. Aunt Lisa stood up, setting her book aside, and walked over, bending down with her hands on her knees. "TJ?" she asked. "Where did you go with your cousin?"

He didn't respond.

Aunt Lisa sighed, straightening out again. "Well, go wash your hands. Dinner should be ready soon. Assuming your daddy doesn't burn down the building."

"I heard that," Uncle Toby called from the balcony.

TJ turned around and silently walked down the hall to the bathroom.

I stood there, staring after him. "I don't understand."

"Don't understand what, sweetheart?" Aunt Lisa asked. She caught me eyeing her book and snatched it up, just as I got a glimpse of the cover. It was a picture of a little boy, probably about TJ's age, with the title *Psychological Trauma and Recovery* across the top in big black letters. Aunt Lisa tucked it into the same cabinet as her binder, before walking over to the table, where her papers were still lying around.

The cabinet called out to me again.

I had to fight it.

But I was sure there were answers hidden in there.

"TJ," I said, stumbling along after her. "He was...he was talking."

"Talking?"

"I swear it."

She looked at me. There was a kind of resignation in her eyes. Like she didn't really believe me. Or couldn't believe me. One of the two. "He isn't completely silent," she said. "We can sometimes get a noise or—"

"It wasn't a noise," I said. "He was talking. *He was talking.*"

She stood there for a moment, eerily quiet. I was almost afraid she was going to call me a liar. Tell me not to make up stories. But she didn't. Instead, her eyes softened. I saw a gleam in them. A light that I might even call hope. "Really?" she asked.

"Really."

"Leah, you don't know how hard it's been to—"

"Really. He *was* talking. You'll see!"

But we didn't see. Not even a little bit. Dinner was a total bust. TJ didn't talk and, of course, he didn't eat a bite. I was a little less worried about that, now that I knew he was eating Michelle's protein bars. But Uncle Toby and Aunt Lisa didn't know that.

And I wasn't sure I could tell them.

Not without unraveling the whole thing.

But as I ate, I watched Aunt Lisa. I watched the hope drain out of her.

And I felt bad. Because I'd given her that hope.

It was my fault.

"Come on, TJ," Uncle Toby said. "I went out and hunted that brontosaurus just for you. Everyone knows a bronto is the tastiest meat."

"Not now, Toby," Aunt Lisa said.

"But it's true, *bubbeleh*."

"No more stories."

Uncle Toby sighed, and he turned his attention back to his plate for a moment. It wasn't really brontosaurus meat. Just turkey burgers and skinless chicken breasts. The healthy foods Ms. Weinstein demanded.

I would have to get my hands on that binder again.

For one thing, I still wasn't sure what healthy foods had to do with anything.

For another, I needed those answers.

The silence was powerful. The only sound was the clink of our forks and knives. And, for me, the echo of memory, of TJ and the way he'd laughed while Michelle chased him around the back room of the laundromat with Francis the flamingo.

If only Uncle Toby and Aunt Lisa could have heard it.

My phone vibrated. Probably Nicole, looking for an update on the whole situation.

And suddenly, I felt so dumb.

My phone! I should have taken it out, when I had the chance. I should have recorded the way TJ was laughing and playing like a normal kid. Like our old Hedgehog. I felt guilty. I owed Uncle Toby and Aunt Lisa the sound of his voice.

It was Violet's fault. She was the one who told me it was rude to take pictures of people without their permission.

She'd made me forget.

Or, at least, that's what I decided to tell myself. Not that I was *really* mad at her.

I didn't get mad. Especially not about little things like that.

"Well," Uncle Toby said, "how's the crafts fair coming, *bubbeleh*?"

As it turned out, Aunt Lisa's summer project was helping to organize the Oak Lake crafts fair. The papers sprawled across the table were applications, vendor information, and maps of Frank Street, divided up into little squares to represent booths for artists. She groaned, letting her head tip back slightly. "Oh, it's such a mess, Toby. I don't know why I volunteered for it."

"You love doing things for the neighborhood."

"I know, I know," she said. "The neighborhood means the world to me. But it's a lot more work than I thought it would be." To say nothing of all the hard work she was putting into trying to get TJ to talk to her. The more I thought about it, the more I realized it was a miracle that Aunt Lisa was still standing. "And I'm just terrified that we're going to go through all of this rigmarole and no one's going to come, anyway."

"What's rigmarole?" I asked.

Aunt Lisa looked over at TJ. "Sweetie, do you want to tell her? Remember? We read that word in the book about the tigers?"

He didn't say a word.

She sighed. "It means 'hassle.' I'm worried that we're

going to go through all the trouble and not get a lot of visitors."

"Why wouldn't they come?" I asked.

"Oak Lake is only one neighborhood," she said. "And a pretty small one at that. And while I personally believe there isn't a better place in the world, Chicago in the summer has a million different fairs and festivals and concerts and, well, you name it, we've got it. Our little shindig might very well get lost in the shuffle."

"I'm sure that won't happen, *bubbeleh*," Uncle Toby said.

"Well, I wish I had your confidence."

"What have you done to advertise the crafts fair?" I asked.

Aunt Lisa looked over at me, as if I'd started speaking another language. "Well, of course, there's an announcement in the *Oak Lake Sentinel*," she said.

"The what?"

Uncle Toby chuckled. "It's this little newsletter that goes out to everyone in the neighborhood," he said.

"Don't call it 'little,' Toby."

He held up his hands in a gesture of surrender. "What do you want me to say? It goes to five hundred people. Tops. In a city that has a population of..."

He faltered.

In a flash, I pulled out my phone and looked it up. "It

says here Chicago has a population of almost three million," I said.

"No phones at the dinner table, Leah," Aunt Lisa said.

Uncle Toby chuckled. "It's what she does."

I put away my phone. "Do you want people from outside of Oak Lake to come to the fair?" I asked.

"Well, of course," Aunt Lisa said.

"Have you done any social media?"

"A bit," she said. "We've got ads on Facebook and Twitter."

"What about Instagram? Tumblr? Plurk? Slack? Discord? And YouTube? Oh, and it's an art fair, so you could also go up on DeviantArt."

"Exactly how many of these platforms do you have?" Aunt Lisa asked.

I shrugged. "None of those yet. Not old enough. But I'm getting them all when I turn thirteen. Maybe you could start a blog about the crafts fair. Get people interested. Coming attractions and stuff. A different artist could write each post. With pictures of their art that'll get people excited to see it. Less work for you that way, too."

"She may be right, *bubbeleh*," Uncle Toby said. "You listen to Leah. She's good at organizing things."

"Oh, she's absolutely the best," Aunt Lisa said. "But it's too much. Everyone on the planning committee is overwhelmed as it is."

"I could do it," I said. "I mean, I'm going to be here for a few weeks. I'd be happy to help out."

"Absolutely not," she said. "It's the summer. I won't be putting any niece of mine to work in the middle of summer."

"But—"

"Besides, you spend too much time online, as it is." She sounded just like my mom. "The crafts fair will be fine," she said. "Don't you worry about it."

"I just want to help."

She reached across the table, putting her hand over mine, giving it a light squeeze. "You're a sweetheart, Leah. But please. It's the summer. While you're here, I want you having fun."

In all honesty, it sounded fun to me. But I knew better than to argue with Aunt Lisa. And, I supposed, now wasn't the time to get distracted. I really had been close to something with TJ. I knew that. Maybe I just had to try again.

I looked over at him, sitting in his enormous chair, staring at his plate, without touching any of the brontosaurus meat. "Hey, Hedgehog?" I said.

He didn't look up.

"Do you want to go for a walk again tomorrow?"

I didn't have expectations. So it was a surprise when he just barely nodded.

If I hadn't been paying close attention, I would have missed it.

Across the table, I thought I heard Aunt Lisa gasp a little. But when I looked at her, she was focused on her own plate, neatly cutting up her turkey burger into little squares. "There we go," she said. "You'll get in some quality time with your cousin."

"Yeah," I said.

Quality time with TJ. And hopefully, Michelle and Violet, too.

And Sir Staples.

I really wanted that part of TJ to come back.

CHAPTER TEN

Michelle kept busy after we left Squeaky Green. And when we arrived the next morning, we saw all of her hard work. Every single one of her boxes of lost treasures was open, sitting on the table, on the counters, and on the floor. Besides the usual buttons and ribbons and candy-bar wrappers, she'd produced a weird assortment of objects from the miscellany box, including a couple of white feathers, a string of dingy yellow lace, and a wad of gray-and-brown dryer lint, about the size of TJ's head.

"What's this?" TJ asked, bounding over to the table to inspect the new finds.

He was talking again, apparently.

"More lost things," Michelle said, balancing on one

foot. Today, she was wearing a sleeveless pink plaid, button-down shirt, tied at her waist, and a pair of jean shorts. One sock was green, with giant white eyes on either side. The other was striped red, orange, and purple. "For Queenie and Staples and Francis."

I ran my finger along the spine of one of the feathers. "These would make decent bumblebee wings," I said, remembering the way we'd diagrammed insect wings in our science class the year before.

Was it exactly the same? No.

But it would work.

They had the *feel* of the wings.

"I was thinking that," Michelle replied. "And this"— she held up the lace—"could be a collar. Like that picture of Queen Elizabeth in Mr. Rosenzweig's classroom, the one with the big dress."

"Oooh, I like that," Violet said.

"I love looking at that dress." Michelle sighed. "I some-times imagine what it would be like to wear it."

Violet smirked. "Why am I not surprised?"

"I'll bet the big skirt has all kinds of secret compart-ments in it. Like an inner pocket filled with grapes."

"Why grapes?" Violet asked.

"In case the queen gets hungry." Michelle giggled. "That's what I'd do if I were Queen Elizabeth."

"Queen Elizabeth?" I said. I remembered the name

from the news. "The lady from England with the funny hats?"

"No, no. That's Queen Elizabeth the Second," Michelle said. "I mean Queen Elizabeth the First. This ancient British queen who wore big, puffy dresses."

We each claimed a seat around the table. Violet slipped Queenie back on her arm, and Michelle and I got down to business, gluing the wings in place. I took out my phone with my free hand to look up a picture of Queen Elizabeth I. And Michelle was right. The lace matched the picture perfectly, on a slightly smaller scale. I helped her glue the dress ruffle in place around Queenie's neck. TJ put Staples on his hand but set his chin on the table, mostly watching the two of us work. It was hard to believe that Queenie was made out of junk. She looked pretty great. After she was dressed, Michelle had Violet stuff some of the dryer lint inside the sock. Queenie's body filled out nicely. She really did look like a round, fluffy bee. Violet buzzed her around the room experimentally.

"What do you think, buddy?" Michelle asked TJ.

"She's great!" he said. "Is it my turn now?"

"I found the perfect nose for a hedgehog," she replied.

And she really had, too. It was a bead that had come off someone's clothes and gotten lodged in the lint trap of one of the dryers. It was shiny and black, just like a real hedgehog nose. We stuffed lint into Staples's snout, then glued the bead to the tip.

"Hold it in place, TJ," Violet said. "The last thing you want is for your hedgehog to have a runny nose."

"Runny nose?" TJ said.

"A nose that runs away. After it falls off."

He laughed at that.

Violet looked pleased.

It seemed like the two of them were getting along much better, now that Violet wasn't taking obsessive notes.

I slipped my phone off the table and tried to angle it up, so I could get a quick snippet of video, but it wasn't working. The table's edge kept blocking the shot.

And I was pretty sure I could feel Violet giving me a pointed look.

I was being rude.

But she didn't get it. She didn't know how much I needed the proof of life from TJ. How much Aunt Lisa and Uncle Toby needed it.

"He needs something to make him a knight, though," TJ said, examining Staples critically.

"What makes someone a knight?" I asked, closing the camera app and setting the phone back on the table in defeat.

Michelle gave us a dreamy smile. "A brave heart."

Another candy-bar wrapper was turned inside out. We cut the shiny, silver paper into the shape of a big heart, then glued it to Staples's chest, like a badge of honor.

TJ beamed.

"What about Francis?" I asked.

"I had an idea about him," Michelle said. She opened a drawer and pulled out a couple of wadded-up, used dryer sheets. "We could color these pink and tear them into strips to be feathers."

"A few on top of his head," Violet said. "He is a hairdresser, after all. You can't have a bald hairdresser."

Michelle nodded. "Exactly."

There were four sheets and four of us. So we sat around the table, and Michelle gave us each a marker. She had what seemed like an endless supply of different shades of pink, since it was her favorite color. "Jamal and I used to draw together all the time."

"Sounds like you *used* to do a lot of things together," Violet said.

Michelle sighed. "I used to be his favorite person in the whole world."

It wasn't quite as easy as drawing on paper. There were all sorts of little dips and crevices in the surface of the sheets. But we were determined, and it was oddly peaceful to just sit and color.

I scrolled through the Wikipedia page on Queen

Elizabeth I as I worked, my curiosity getting the better of me. Her royal motto—apparently, old kings and queens had their own mottos—was "I see but say nothing." Sounded like TJ.

One click led to another.

The way it always did.

And as I was scrolling through an article about the Shelby Gem Factory (after clicking on Tower of London, Crown Jewels of England, Black Prince's Ruby, and rubies), TJ looked up at Michelle.

"Hey, Michelle?" he said. There was a trip of hesitation in his voice.

Michelle looked at him. "Yeah?"

"Do you think..."

"What?"

"Do you think that you could...maybe..."

"Maybe what?" She paused. "Buddy, I can't do anything unless you tell me what it is. I don't have my psychic license yet."

TJ shrugged one shoulder up to his ear, squirming in his seat. "Do you think you could maybe tell Violet and Leah the story?" he asked.

"The story?" I said, my fingers hesitating.

Violet raised both eyebrows. "What story?"

But Michelle didn't look at either of us. She widened her eyes, staring at TJ. "*The* story?" she said.

"Yes," he said.

"Whaaaaaaat stooooooory?" Violet repeated.

"Really, TJ?" Michelle said, ignoring her. "You want me to tell them *the* story?"

"Yes, please."

"I don't know." She pursed her lips together. I could tell that she was just teasing TJ, but he thought she was being very serious. "Do you think they'd believe it?"

"Yes," he said. No hitch in his voice. He was certain. In a way I hadn't seen him be certain about anything, all week.

"And you think they're worthy of hearing it?"

He nodded. "I think so."

Michelle took a deep breath, then let it out slowly, giving him a solemn nod. "Well, all right. But only because you trust them."

"What's the story?" Violet asked.

"It's a secret," Michelle said. "Passed down from laundromat owner to laundromat owner, since the beginning of time."

"Which was a long, long time ago," TJ said.

"I would never have guessed," Violet said dryly.

I kicked her under the table.

"Ow!"

"It's about another world," Michelle continued. "A world that most people don't even know about."

"Tell them what it's called," TJ said.

She glanced sideways at him. "I'm getting there, I'm getting there." I got the sense that she was kind of enjoying his impatience.

Violet set her chin in her palm, elbow resting on the table. "Oh, I am all ears for this," she said.

Ever the journalist. Ever ready to hear the scoop. Even without her notebook.

"Another world?" I asked.

"A parallel universe to ours," Michelle said. She held out both of her hands, her palms just centimeters apart. "Touching in places, but only just touching. It's called..." She paused. It was the same sort of dramatic pause that Uncle Toby used in the middle of one of his CIA stories. The kind of pause that made everyone listening eager for the story to continue. "The Land of Lost Things."

"Well, that's a mouthful," Violet said.

"The Land of Lost Things." I looked at TJ as I said it.

He was staring up at Michelle, with an expression I didn't entirely understand. It was equal parts awe and excitement. And a sort of longing. There was a need, a desire in his shining eyes.

"There are gateways to it in this very building," Michelle continued. "You see, the best way to reach the Land of Lost Things is through the back wall of a dryer."

The word fell like a thud in the middle of the room.

I turned to her. "A dryer?"

"Of course," she said. "Haven't you ever noticed how things sometimes just disappear from the laundry?"

As she said it, I turned to look at the piles and piles of socks on the table. All of them lost, without a partner. "I guess so," I said.

"They don't just"—she snapped her fingers—"vanish into thin air, you know. They go somewhere. They're transported."

"To the Land of Lost Things," Violet said.

"Exactly! And socks are only the beginning of it. There are so many things that people just lose. Because they're careless or thoughtless or just not paying attention."

"Or because they're mean," TJ added.

I looked at him. "Mean?"

Michelle kept going. "If you visit the Land of Lost Things, you'll find an entire ocean, filled with nothing but pens and earrings and buttons and half-used lipsticks."

"And socks," Violet said.

"Of course! Socks, too. Keys. Homework assignments."

"Mittens," Violet added. "My sister loses at least one every winter."

Michelle snapped her fingers again and pointed at Violet. "Yes!"

"Tell them about the castle," TJ said.

"I'm getting to it. Just a second." Michelle grinned

at us. "But yes. He's right. There's a palace in the Land of Lost Things. A beautiful palace, made of white marble and gold, with columns as big as trees. And a courtyard blooming with a thousand flowers that were given to girls for school dances and accidentally left behind in the bathroom."

"Tell them where it comes from! The castle! That's the most important part!"

She looked down at TJ. "Do *you* want to tell the story?" she asked.

TJ shook his head. "No. I can't tell stories like you do."

Michelle's smile got so big I figured it had to be hurting her cheeks. "The palace is ancient. Older than the oldest castle in England or France or China. It wasn't built in the Land of Lost Things, you see. The reason why it came to be there is because the palace itself was lost."

Violet raised both her eyebrows. "How do you lose a castle? I mean, they're big." She gestured to her face with her marker. "Most people have eyes."

"It's the castle from Atlantis," Michelle said.

We both fell silent for a moment. Violet blinked. And then, as I watched, a slow smile spread across her face. "Atlantis," she said. "The *lost* continent."

"Yup."

"I get it," she said.

"The Land of Lost Things is a mysterious place."

"An immortal place," I said suddenly. I don't know why. I guess I just wanted to be part of it. "After all, you know what we lose way too often?"

"What?" Violet asked.

"Time. We're always losing time."

I had heard the expression before. "Lost time." And "losing track of time," too. I did it constantly, whenever an internet search started to spiral out of control. But I'd never really thought of it as something concrete. Not until I was suddenly invited into Michelle's imaginary world.

"I guess," Violet said.

"Time doesn't move in the Land of Lost Things," I said. "It's always both day and night. The sun and moon sharing the sky."

TJ's eyes widened. "So you *know* about the Land of Lost Things?" he asked.

"Sure," Violet said. "Of course she does." She gestured around the table. "All three of us do. In fact, all seventh graders know about the Land of Lost Things."

"Really?"

Violet seemed to be having fun. "Yeah. Tell him about it, Leah."

Michelle and Violet both turned to me. The words came to me effortlessly, like they'd been waiting for me my whole life. "You know, you can never *get lost* in the Land of Lost Things," I said. "You always find your way to whatever you want to see; you don't even need a map. Because people only lose their way here. In fact, every time someone here gets lost, their sense of direction just flies over to the Land of Lost Things, and someone there is able to find their way."

TJ was staring, his little mouth hanging open.

"And the *Titanic* is there," I said. "It sank through the bottom of the ocean and out of our world. It sails the seas of the Land of Lost Things."

"With Amelia Earhart at the ship's helm," Michelle said. "She was lost hundreds of years ago."

"Who?" TJ asked.

"Amelia Earhart," Michelle said. "The famous aviator."

Violet tilted her head to one side. "What's an aviator?"

"An airplane pilot," TJ said.

"Right!" Michelle said with a grin. "She tried to fly all the way around the world, but one day, her plane completely vanished. Poof!"

"Because it slipped into the Land of Lost Things," Violet said.

"Exactly!"

TJ's eyes danced from Michelle to Violet to me and back again.

"But, of course," Violet said, "Amelia sails her ship under the flag of the queen of the Land of Lost Things."

"Who's that?" TJ asked.

"Why, Queen Queenie the bumblebee."

TJ wrinkled his nose. "But she's just a puppet."

"A puppet based on the actual queen," Michelle said. "Violet only had one sock to make her. The other's off in the Land of Lost Things. Sitting on the throne."

He considered it a moment and then slowly nodded, accepting the explanation, even though it seemed flimsy to me. "I guess that makes sense," he said. "Does that mean there's a Sir Staples there, too? And Francis the royal hairdresser?"

"Of course," I said.

"You know," Michelle said, "since we're all in on the secret, I think that maybe we should start a club."

"A club?" I asked.

She nodded. "A special club."

I shivered with delight at the word.

Special.

"What do we call ourselves?" TJ asked.

"The Lost Things Club."

There was no better name. We all found ourselves nodding in silent agreement. "But a club needs to be more than just a club," Violet said. "We have to have a charter."

"A charter?" Michelle said. "What's that?"

"A reason for existing," she said. "Something that makes us special."

That word again. *Special.*

"Maybe some kind of shared mission."

Violet was on a roll. "Well," Michelle said, "that should be obvious."

TJ looked at her. "What's our charter?"

"It's our sacred honor and duty to tell the story of the Land of Lost Things," Michelle said, touching a hand solemnly to her heart. "So the story itself doesn't get lost."

"Oh, yes." Violet copied her, putting a hand to her heart as well. "Yes, of course. It's an important job. For the future of history itself." She looked at TJ. "What do you think?"

"I don't know," TJ said, scrunching up his face a little bit.

Michelle tilted her head, the keys in her hair clacking against one another. "You don't want to be in a club?"

"Of course I do!" TJ said.

"So what's the problem?"

"How do we...how do we follow our charter?" he asked. "How do we tell people about the Land of Lost Things? They won't believe us, will they?"

Violet and Michelle looked at each other. And I could tell that neither of them were sure how to answer. The story and the conversation and the club. We all knew why it was happening. It was for TJ. TJ, who only seemed to come alive in the presence of lost things. There was no question that he was troubled. We'd all seen the way he acted when he wasn't at Squeaky Green. Even Michelle. She probably knew best of all. She'd seen when he ran away from Ms. Weinstein.

She took such good care of him. Like a big sister.

Now I understood. Everything Michelle did, everything she said, and the way she looked after him. It was all about TJ. She had somehow realized that TJ needed this, needed the Land of Lost Things.

And if that's what he needed, that's what he would get.

"I think I know," I said, rippling my fingers.

All at once, I knew a lot of things. Including my role in all of this.

I guess that's just how inspiration comes. Without warning. It just hits you. Like lightning or pigeon droppings.

TJ looked at me eagerly. "You do?"

"Of course," I said. "I know exactly how we share the story of the Land of Lost Things with the world."

"How?"

I picked up my phone.

CHAPTER ELEVEN

We added pink dryer sheet feathers to Francis. Two elegant plumes on top of his head and more down the length of his neck. And used lint to extend his beak, running an orange ribbon around the back of it to give it that flamingo ombré, from orange to black. Someone had left a plastic comb in their pocket, sending it through a washing machine. We pulled off the long, black teeth, curling them with our fingers and gluing them over Francis's eyes one at a time, giving him thick, luxurious lashes.

Sir Staples received buckteeth, made out of two pieces of gum. To soften the look of his quills, we wrapped loose pieces of yarn in black and brown and gray around the pens. It made him fuller and fuzzier. More like something you'd want to cuddle. Less like an office-supply store had exploded.

I donated my blond hair extensions to Queenie. Michelle carefully looped them under her crown.

Michelle's mom came in around noon, the sound of the door opening startling us all, especially TJ. But Michelle's mom was no less startled to see so many kids hanging out with Michelle.

"Hi, Mama," Michelle said.

"What's all this?" she asked.

"Just hanging out with my friends."

"Your friends?" Michelle's mom grinned. "That's wonderful. About time you brought some friends around!"

"Is Jamal here?"

Her mom shook her head. "You know I can't get that boy to come out of his room. I don't know what I'm going to do about him."

Michelle's shoulders sagged. But she didn't say anything.

"Listen, I need to drive Willy to his basketball thing in Skokie, so I just came back to grab my purse. Are you kids hungry?"

We were. And she offered to order a pizza. Unfortunately, we couldn't agree on a topping.

Violet wanted green peppers and olives.

Michelle wanted pineapple and spinach.

I wanted sausage and onion.

TJ wanted pepperoni.

We settled on plain cheese.

And, as luck would have it, we decided that the plastic table, the one used to keep the top of the delivery box from touching the cheese, would be perfect for the inside of Queenie's crown, which had started to collapse in on itself. The white spokes of it towered over the silver teeth of the crown. Michelle found a couple of brightly colored beads and glued them to the tops. They looked like precious jewels.

"You're so good at seeing how things can work together," Violet said. It was a rare compliment.

Michelle shrugged. "When we were little, I had to keep Jamal entertained. It's all about adapting. You'd be amazed how just a ring of keys can keep a toddler happy for hours."

By the time we were ready, the table was covered with Michelle's boxes and socks. It was messy, but I wanted it that way. I wanted a jumble of confused shapes and colors. A swimming sea of lost things, so mixed and matched that it was hard to tell where one thing ended and the next one began. All part of the bigger picture forming in my mind. "Go to the other side of the table," I told them, once we were sure the glue on the puppets was dry.

The three of them obeyed.

"Now," I continued, "you have to squat down, so that your heads are all under the edge of the table."

"Like this?" TJ asked, dropping down to his haunches.

"Perfect," I said.

"Easy for him to do," Violet said, crouching. "He's a little pip-squeak. Some of us are over four feet tall."

It took her a bit of maneuvering before she was able to get it so the top of her head didn't show.

"All right," I said. "Now, all of you, hold up your puppets."

Queenie, Francis, and Sir Staples appeared, like they'd risen out of the sea on the table itself.

The lost things had come alive.

"Oh, that's perfect!" I said. I took out my phone, opening up the video app. When I held the camera up, I saw an awesome picture. Staples and Francis were evenly centered. "Violet, move Queenie a little closer to Francis."

Grumbling, Violet scooted closer to Michelle on the floor.

In the frame, Queenie came into focus.

"That looks great!"

"Wonderful!" Violet said. "Now what?"

"Now, I guess we begin filming."

"We need something to say," she replied.

"Oh." I frowned. "Uh, I don't know." How did these things usually begin? I quickly thought through all the YouTube channels I watched, with all their gimmicks and hooks. When I thought about it, they all really began the exact same way. There was a formula they followed. And I'd watched so many, I kind of knew it by heart. "I guess you can start by introducing yourselves," I said. "Or, at least, your puppets."

"Don't forget the charter, Leah," TJ chimed in.

"What?"

"The charter! We have to tell the story."

"Oh, right!" I said. "That should come next." The way all the YouTubers introduced their channels.

"Should Staples tell it?" Michelle asked.

"No," TJ said. "I think Francis should."

"Why Francis?" Violet asked.

"I like his funny voice."

"What voice?" Michelle asked. And then she immediately went into her over-the-top accent. "Blimey! Do you mean this voice here, me old chum?"

"Yes."

She giggled. "All right."

"And then what?" Violet asked.

"And then..." Michelle paused. I couldn't see her under the table, but my guess was that she was twisting her mouth up to one side.

"The charter," I said. "And then we ask everyone watching to spread the story. That's how it gains power. From being told."

"Really?" TJ asked.

"Really. And all good videos end with the people in them asking the people watching to look out for more," I said.

"Well, I think that sounds like a job for Queen Queenie," Violet said.

TJ made Staples dance in the air. "Yes, yes, yes!" he said.

"All right." I held up my camera. "Let's do this."

"How do we know when to start?" Michelle asked.

"In the movies," TJ said, "they always go 'Lights! Camera! Action!'"

I nodded. "I'll do that, then. Okay?"

"Yup."

"Okay!"

"Sounds good!"

My finger hovered eagerly over the record button. With a smile, I stared into the screen. "Lights! Camera! Action!"

We thought it would be easy, but, of course, we were so very wrong. Even figuring out who would say which part was difficult. Without a script, Francis, Queenie, and Staples kept talking over each other. I had to stop the camera every time. In fact, the first few takes lasted five seconds at most before two people tried to talk at the same time.

"Let's take a step back," I said, after nearly ten mess-ups. "Before we film, let's try to rehearse it a little bit."

"What's rehearse?" TJ asked.

"Practice." How many times had I heard Nicole talking about the theatre? Clearly enough that it had sunk in, at least a little.

And rehearsing turned out to be a wise decision. It definitely helped smooth out some of the bumps, anyway.

"Greetings from the Land of Lost Things!" the three of them all said, speaking together as one, after we agreed that was how to start.

"I'm Queen Queenie the Fifth!"

"I'm Sir Staples!"

"And I'm Francis the flamingo."

Just that little bit, those opening moments, took us about an hour to figure out. We rehearsed and rehearsed until it was perfect. And then realized that we had a whole lot more of the video to go.

We couldn't be perfect. Not if we wanted to finish it before dinner.

We'd have to settle for "good enough."

After that, things got easier. We broke the video down into three different pieces. The beginning, middle, and end.

"Timeless classics," as Violet called them with a glimmer of amusement.

We practiced each part on its own.

And then started trying to string them all together.

The hardest part was learning how to keep going, even when someone said something wrong or silly or out of place. TJ was particularly bothered by that.

Once, while Francis was in the middle of explaining the Land of Lost Things, Violet chuckled and said, "There's also a hand lost up my spine!"

"Quit goofing around," TJ snapped, in his own voice, not as Staples.

Another time, when Queenie was encouraging people to follow our adventures, she threw in: "And if you don't want to join us, you can just *get lost*."

"Don't be mean!" TJ said. "If you're mean, you'll pay for it."

"Calm down, TJ," Michelle said. "She was only playing with words."

I couldn't exactly see him, but I was pretty sure that he was pouting. I'd have to talk to him about that. Pouting *never* worked. I'd learned that the hard way, back when I was a little kid. It was almost as bad as crying.

We got through it once. And then again. And looking at the clock, we saw that we'd lost track of time.

"It's now or never," Violet said, lowering her arm to shake out the stiffness in her elbow.

"We got this," Michelle said.

And she was right.

I filmed the whole thing. One straight shot. No one slipped up. No one coughed or sneezed. When someone stumbled over what they were saying, they kept going, without apologizing or "breaking character," another term I'd picked up from Nicole.

Michelle was by far the best.

When Francis started to tell the story, it almost carried me away. In spite of his funny voice and the way he bounced around on screen, his words were hypnotic.

"Nothing's really gone forever. Only misplaced. Lost. And lost things have a whole world of their own, our world. The Land of Lost Things. Remember that blanket you lost on the bus when you were three? Or that book you never meant to leave behind on the train? And that favorite pair of socks, the one that started as two before being separated in the wash? They're all here with us. A part of us. And when your world touches ours, those things touch yours. So fear not for that missing pen, that misplaced retainer, that old, forgotten key chain. They've found their way home."

Home.

If only lost things really did have a home.

When we finished, I called, "Cut!" And all three of them let out a whoop.

"We did it!" Michelle said, jumping up to her feet.

"That was so cool!" TJ said.

Violet stood up, putting her hands on her hips and bending her back over, stretching out the cricks in her spine. "Of course," she said, "you realize this means we're going to have to film more. I mean, we promised our viewers more adventures."

"If we actually get any viewers," Michelle said.

"I know how to get to work on that, at least," I said.

"Where are you going to put it?"

"YouTube," I said.

You couldn't have a YouTube account if you were under thirteen. Since I was only twelve, I didn't have my own. But my mom had an account: HannahCantor777. One she almost never used, so I logged in to that. In the past, she'd let me post some videos from trips we'd taken. Sweeping panoramas of New York City and Aspen and Los Angeles. I was allowed to post anything I wanted, as long as it didn't have my face in it. Or TJ's face.

Sir Staples didn't count.

So I uploaded the video.

"'The Land of Lost Things. Part One'?" I looked at the others as I filled in the title.

"Part one," Violet said. She looked at Michelle.

Michelle nodded. "Part one."

Part one it would be. With a few keystrokes, I put it out into the world. And then I texted the link to Nicole. I owed her a picture for the day, and this was even better than a picture.

"That was so much fun, you guys!" TJ said. His eyes were shining.

Violet ruffled his hair. "Glad you enjoyed it."

"But we're running out of time," I added. "We need to be back for dinner in twenty minutes."

"Help me pack up some of this stuff," Michelle said. "Don't worry about the socks, though. I'll take care of that."

We put away the extra buttons and beads and ribbons. Well, Michelle, TJ, and I did. Violet decided to start alphabetizing the shoeboxes, so she kept taking them out when we put them in, rearranging the order, muttering under her breath about how we needed to have a list to find things in the future.

"Hey, Michelle?" TJ said, as he carefully set Staples down on the table, like he was putting a baby to sleep in a crib.

She looked over at him. "Yeah?"

"When are we going to get to go to the Land of Lost Things?"

"Go there?" Violet said.

"Michelle told me we could go there sometime."

"Why would you want to?"

163

He turned his eyes away from her, and I thought I could see a little color rise in his chubby cheeks.

"Soon, TJ," Michelle said, tossing her hair and the keys over one shoulder, with a lovely jingle.

"When?"

"I said, 'soon.'"

"But what does that mean?"

"When the time is right."

"How do we know when that is?"

"If I had something more specific, I'd say it."

TJ scowled. "Before school starts again?"

"Oh, definitely," she replied.

"Good." He nodded. "We have to go before school starts. I need to go before school starts."

"Of course," Michelle said.

I glanced at the clock in the corner of my phone screen, then held a hand out to TJ. "Come on, Hedgehog, we have to get home."

He walked over to me. Slowly. Reluctantly.

"Violet?" I said. "You coming?"

"You go ahead without me," Violet said. "I want to finish organizing these boxes."

Behind her, Michelle rolled her eyes.

"Okay," I said, taking TJ by the hand.

We left Squeaky Green together, the regular customers smiling at TJ.

He smiled back.

At first.

But the smile thinned. And by the time we'd stepped outside into the warm and wet evening air, the smile had faded completely.

I knew what was going to happen.

He was going to slip away. Bit by bit. Until we got back to Uncle Toby and Aunt Lisa's apartment. And there would be nothing left of the sunny boy I'd spent the day with.

Well. Nothing but the video, anyway.

"Hey, little man!" Morgan called to us, as we crossed under the bridge. He was wiping down the counter in front of the doughnut shop.

"Hi, Morgan," TJ replied.

"How are you, Cousin?" he asked.

I felt a little heat rise in my cheeks. I didn't think I'd ever feel comfortable talking to a stranger, even if TJ did. "Fine," I mumbled, staring straight ahead.

"It's okay," TJ whispered to me, once we passed under the tracks and out of earshot. "Morgan's safe."

I looked down at him. "Yeah?"

"Promise."

"You seem to like him. Why is that, Hedgehog?"

TJ shrugged. "I just do."

"There has to be a reason."

"I don't know," he said. "I guess he's the only grown-up who doesn't ask me how I'm feeling all the time."

"Oh."

I didn't know what to make of that. Then again, I'd caught a glimpse of Aunt Lisa's articles, all those lists about taking care of a child and listening to him and asking him questions. Aunt Lisa was always hovering around TJ. Uncle Toby, too. I guess I could see how that might get exhausting after a while.

I wondered if I counted as a "grown-up."

I hoped not.

And that was kind of funny. Usually, I was sick of people treating me like a kid. But just this once, I guess I needed to be one.

"Hey, Hedgehog?" I said.

He looked up at me. "Yeah?"

"Are you okay?"

He shrugged.

"You know, if something's making you sad, you could tell me."

TJ looked away.

At first, I didn't think I'd get a reply. We were close to home. His step was heavier. And his focus drifting. The shine was gone from his eyes now. They were colorless again.

But right before we climbed the stairs, he shook his

head, ever so slightly. "I just want to visit the Land of Lost Things," he said. "Soon."

That was the end of it.

He didn't say a single word the rest of the night.

But after TJ and Uncle Toby and Aunt Lisa went to bed for the night, I sat on the sleeper sofa in the study, playing the video we'd made again and again. Just to hear his voice.

And trying to see something more.

A bigger picture.

A puzzle.

One I couldn't put together yet.

CHAPTER TWELVE

The funny thing was, it turned out that I wasn't the only person watching the video. When I woke up the next morning, I had fifteen text messages waiting for me. The first was from Nicole:

> That video is crazy cute. Shared it with
> everyone at camp!

It was sweet. I thanked her with two heart emojis: one purple, because that was my favorite color, and one orange, because that was her favorite color.

Then, I quickly realized that Nicole must have shown it to more than just her camp friends, because the other fourteen texts were from our classmates. No one I was especially close to: kids who were in the school play with Nicole, Nicole's next-door neighbor, even David, the boy Nicole had a crush on. All of them said more or less the same thing:

> **So cute!**
>
> **I love it!**
>
> **More please!**
>
> **Francis is my hero!**
>
> **Leah, you should totally join the film and theatre club!**

Honestly, I didn't know what to do with all that attention. I was just glad none of them could see me. I was blushing uncontrollably.

I thanked all of them.

After that, I went to YouTube and saw that over a thousand people had viewed the video already. In less than sixteen hours. That was more than any video of mine. Probably more than all of them combined. We had thirty-six thumbs-up and zero thumbs-down, so far. It was unbelievable. Like all my classmates had sent it to their friends, who had sent it on to their friends. I let out a tiny squeal of delight.

There were even comments, too:

How did you make those puppets?

Are the puppets actual lost things?

Someone should put this on cable access!

Is that Squeaky Green in Oak Lake?

That last comment made my heart jump. We'd been so careful not to let anyone know who we were. But peering into the corner of the screen, I realized that there was an old Squeaky Green sign up on the wall in the back room.

I was going to have to pay more attention to the bigger picture. That one was on me.

The comment went on:

That neighborhood's had a rough couple of months. Great to see something so sweet coming out of it! Yay!

Uncle Toby had the day off and said he wanted to join us for our walk. TJ gave me a look, so fast that Uncle Toby missed it. It was a look of panic. A look of fear. And a look that said he needed me. He needed me desperately.

And he needed to keep Squeaky Green our secret.

I suggested we go to the park.

The three of us ended up sitting side by side by side on a wooden bench, watching the neighborhood kids play a game of pickup basketball.

"Did I ever tell you about the time the CIA had to play a winner-takes-all game of basketball with a team of aliens from the planet Cattatoon Eight?" Uncle Toby asked us, taking a sly sip of his pop. "The fate of the entire human race was at stake."

I smiled absently and refreshed YouTube to see that the video was up to forty-one thumbs-up.

Saturday was more of the same. But on Sunday, I woke up to a silent house. Uncle Toby had to take the car into the garage, and Aunt Lisa went to church. They left me a note saying they'd be back in the afternoon and told me to watch over TJ.

By this point, the video had climbed up to three thousand views. We had fifty-eight thumbs-up and only one thumbs-down. New comments popped up, all of them excited and encouraging, from people I didn't know, with avatars I'd never even seen before. I showed TJ when he crept out of his room, wiping sleep away from his eyes.

"Is that good?" he asked me softly.

"That's incredible."

And you know what was even more incredible? Hearing him talk in the apartment!

"You know what that means?" he said.

"I'm ten steps ahead of you, Hedgehog," I told him.

I was already texting Violet.

Meet us at Squeaky Green. We have work to do.

I texted Uncle Toby and Aunt Lisa to let them know we were going for another walk. And within an hour, Violet, TJ, and I were heading to the train tracks. Just as we were about to pass under, though, Michelle came trotting down the sidewalk, holding a canvas bag that was suspiciously lumpy.

Today's outfit was the most lost of lost things yet.

A ratty, old T-shirt for a Grateful Dead concert. Whatever that was. A pair of scruffy jeans, with one leg cut off at the knee. A knee-high argyle sock on one foot. A short, dainty pink ankle sock with lace around the top on the other.

"Hi there," she said.

"Hi."

"Hey."

"Hiya, Michelle!"

"What are you doing out here?" Violet asked.

Michelle turned her face up to the sky. The sunlight streamed down on her skin, lighting her silhouette a delicate white-gold. My fingers itched to take a picture; it was such a gorgeous moment. "It's such a beautiful day!" she said. And she went up on one leg, spinning around in a lopsided circle, the bag beating against her shoulder. "If you looked up the phrase 'beautiful day' on your phone, you'd see a picture of today!"

It was, in fact, one of those rare summer days in Chicago. When it was neither too hot nor too sticky. It was kind of perfect. Sunny, but with a breeze. We weren't sweating or steaming. The kind of day you wished you could have forever.

"But we have to do another video!" TJ said. "Our charter, remember? It's our duty! We have to tell the story."

Michelle smiled at him. "Who says we have to tell the story only from one place?" she asked.

With that, she opened up the bag and pulled out Staples, his silver heart gleaming in the sun.

"What?" TJ said. "Out here?"

"Why not?"

"But the Land of Lost Things. You get there through a dryer."

"That's only the most obvious entrance," Michelle said. "There are entrances everywhere. Which means, we really ought to *be* everywhere."

173

I could see that Michelle was thinking on her feet. She was good. Really, really good.

TJ didn't look like he was entirely convinced, though. "Like where?" he asked.

Violet jumped in. "Like there." She pointed to a sewer grate, sunken into the curb by the sidewalk.

"Really?"

"Sure!" Michelle said.

TJ turned, immediately rushing over to the grate. He wrapped his tiny fists around two of the metal bars and gave them a sharp tug. Of course, the grate didn't budge.

"You can't get in through there, buddy," Michelle said. "That thing is way too heavy."

"Oh," he said, looking a little disappointed.

"Let's make a video, okay?"

"All right..."

Once Violet, TJ, and Michelle slipped on their puppets, they all turned to look at me. "Where's the best place to film?" Violet asked.

Because, of course, a decision like that fell to me.

That was how I fit in.

That was my place.

"Good question," I said, nibbling on the tip of my tongue. Definitely not at the sewer grate. There was no way to hide their faces there. "If we're telling stories about the Land of Lost Things, then we should probably try to find a lost..."

It hit me without warning, like inspiration always does.

Without saying a word, I moved past them all, marching into the cool shade under the tracks.

"Leah?" Michelle called.

"Where are you going?" Violet asked.

But they followed me. Followed me as I went right for the old, rusty bike. The one I'd taken shelter behind when I was spying on TJ. It was still there. Twisted and rotted, with a spiderweb glittering like silver thread.

"This is it," I said.

"This is a tetanus shot waiting to happen," Violet replied, giving the bike a look, as though it was about to spring like a snake and bite her.

"Trust me, this'll work perfectly."

"Are you sure?"

"Of course."

"It's perfect," Michelle said.

TJ bobbed his head in agreement. "Yeah."

I started experimenting with ways to line up the shot. The bike wasn't as solid and sturdy as the table. I knew I had to find a way to angle the camera so that I saw the puppets but not the puppeteers. So I had the others try a lot of different postures and poses. And just when we were on the verge of giving up, the idea hit me.

"How about I put the bag between the handlebars?" I said, pointing to Michelle's canvas bag. "Then, the

puppets can come up, out of it. Like they're in the basket!"
I was pretty sure I could frame it just so.

"Let's give it a try," Violet said.

And it worked. Somehow, I saw what wasn't there and made it so. It was a little bit of a tight squeeze for the three of them, huddling down around the front wheel. But if I stood on the bottom bar of the next-door bike rack and angled the camera down, zooming in good and close, I could just get all the puppets in the shot, without anyone's arms or faces showing up.

Of course, it was only a momentary victory.

"What are we going to say this time?" TJ asked.

Violet, Michelle, and I each looked at the other.

That was the hardest part.

"Is that my little man, over there?"

The four of us whipped around to spot Morgan. He was hidden in the shade of the doughnut shop, carefully laying out rows of shiny, fresh doughnuts with his gloved hands. The frosting gleamed jewel-bright under the little shop's lights.

"Hi, Morgan," TJ said.

"You bring any bottle caps for me today?" He was extremely precise, I noticed, with his work. Each dough-nut was lovingly lifted out of its pink box, carefully placed. They were evenly spaced, the rows perfectly lined up.

I wanted to take a picture of them.

"No," TJ admitted.

"I'll check for any later today," Michelle said. "Are those the triple chocolate specials?"

"You bet. Hey. What's that you got there?" Morgan asked, pointing to Francis on her arm, as she trotted over to get a better look at the doughnuts.

"That's Francis the flamingo," TJ said, trailing behind Michelle. "And this is Sir Staples! Knight to Queen Queenie. The bravest hedgehog in the whole universe!" Proudly, he pranced Staples across the line of Michelle's shoulders, nuzzling against her neck.

Michelle giggled and raised one leg.

"Queen Queenie?" Morgan said, carefully placing the last doughnut. "What's she queen of?"

"The Land of Lost Things," TJ said.

"Land of Lost Things?"

"Yup."

"Where's that?"

"It's a secret world," he said. "It's where lost things go."

Morgan made a little harrumph. "Lost things, huh?"

"Yup."

"Guess that makes me one of the escapees," Morgan said.

Michelle frowned thoughtfully, tilting her head so her keys jingled against her shoulder. "What's an escapee?"

"It's someone who got away from something," Violet said, walking over.

177

Wide-eyed, TJ turned to look at Morgan again. "You escaped from the Land of Lost Things?"

Morgan nodded, collapsing the empty box and stashing it somewhere behind the register counter in front of him. "Sure did. After all, old Morgan is a genuine lost thing myself."

He was smiling as he said it. An eerie half smile, front tooth jagged and chipped. I felt something rise up from deep inside me. A swell of emotion that I quickly had to force back down. I wasn't going to let myself cry. But I realized that I was, in fact, kind of sad. For Morgan. I didn't know where he came from. But obviously, it wasn't anyplace good. If it were, he wouldn't say he was lost.

He wouldn't look so lonely all the time.

That was no way for a person to live at all.

"Hey, hey!" TJ said. "I think I have an idea for what our next video could be."

"What?" Michelle asked.

"We should talk to Morgan!"

"TJ..." Violet started.

"No, really!" TJ hopped Staples over the air, coming up to Morgan's side. "He could tell us the story about how he escaped from the Land of Lost Things."

"Oh, it's quite the story," Morgan said. He opened a door in the counter, coming out around it with his milk crate, which he set in front of the shop. "Let me tell you."

"Please!" TJ turned to look at me and Michelle. "What do you think? Wouldn't that be a great video?"

I didn't know what to say.

"Sure," Michelle said, deciding for us. "That could be interesting. Queen Queenie could hear the tale of his adventure. And maybe make him a knight."

"Sir Morgan of the Maple Glaze?" Violet said.

"Something like that."

I looked at Morgan. "Morgan, do you want to do this? You don't have to."

He looked over at me, with a softness I hadn't seen in him before. "I'd love to tell a story," he said, his voice quivering just slightly.

Like no one had ever asked him to before.

Like he had been waiting all his life for someone to ask.

Normally, I would have made a face at a grown-up who sounded like he was going to cry. But not this time.

"Well, that settles it," Michelle said. "Let's figure out how we want to film this."

We remembered the lessons we'd learned from our first video. Immediately, we broke the story down into three parts: the beginning, middle, and end. The beginning, I decided, should stay more or less the same as last time. "In case someone only sees the second video, but not the first." Things were always out of order on YouTube. The middle would be the story of Morgan's daring escape.

And then the end would be similar to the first video, with a promise of further adventures to come. But first, Queen Queenie would take a moment to knight Sir Morgan (of the Maple Glaze).

Morgan patiently watched us rehearse our opening, the puppets popping out of the canvas bag on the bike. He actually seemed to enjoy it. Between customers buying doughnut holes and crullers, he laughed at the funny voices Violet, TJ, and Michelle made. And each time, without fail, even if they messed up, he gave them a round of applause at the end.

Nicole would have called it a "standing ovation."

In fifteen minutes, we had the opening down.

Next was the hard part. Or, at least, what I thought would be hard. The telling of Morgan's tale.

"Okay," I said, taking charge, "so I think what we should start with is Francis telling Queenie and Staples that they're going to have a very special visitor."

"Your Majesty, Your Majesty!" Michelle said, going into her Francis voice. "I have magnifisome news! A wandering hero has a tale to tell!"

"Good," I said. "Let's do something like that."

"Okay."

"'Magnifisome' isn't a word," Violet said under her breath.

Michelle stuck out her tongue.

I pointed to TJ. "And you can introduce him."

"How should I do that?" he asked.

"Say something like 'He once was a citizen of our land but braved many dangers to return home.'"

TJ considered it a moment. And then nodded. In his Staples voice, he said, "He was lost in our land. But then he found a way back h-home."

It wasn't word-for-word, but it was close enough.

"Okay," I said. "And then Queenie can say—"

"Bzzzz," Violet interrupted. "Bzzzz. I should very much like to hear the tale of his heroics and name him a knight of my realm!"

"Perfect."

They practiced it three times through. TJ stumbled a little with his wording. Something about the word "home" kept tripping him up. But he knew what he was doing, more or less. He'd get it right.

"What's next?" Violet asked.

"Next is Morgan's story," I said. I looked over at Morgan, who was smoothing down his rumpled, wrinkled apron. "You can tell them the story of how you escaped the Land of Lost Things. How you got back here." I paused. "Do you have any ideas about how—"

"In a flying machine," Morgan said.

TJ looked up at him. "A flying machine?"

"A flying machine I built myself." Morgan settled down

on his milk crate, pulling one of his knees up against his chest with his crooked fingers. I noticed one of his fingers had a pale band of skin around it, like he usually wore a ring, when he wasn't busy selling doughnuts. "You see, I used to be a knight of another land. This land. Our land. A soldier. They said I was a hero. I was the best at building things. Quickly. Sometimes out of nothing at all. Give me the carburetor off a four-by-four truck, a wire hanger, and a piece of gum, and I could whip up something that made toast, hummed 'Baby I Need Your Loving,' and polished your boots at the same time. In a minute or two. Throw in a bottle cap and it would also pick up radio from as far as Abu Dhabi.

"It was a flying machine that carried me here. I built the cabin out of an old bathtub. The kind they used to have, way back when. The kind with feet. And I put a boot on each foot. Strapped to the bottom of the tub were a thousand bottles of hair spray. They were only half-empty. But the rich ladies who bought them threw them out before finishing them up. That was the key to the escape, you see. I needed something for propulsion. I tied a string around the spray buttons and pulled it up through the drain of my tub. And once I was inside, with an old blanket over my head, I pulled the string and ... *vroosh!* The hair spray let loose, spraying all at once. And the force of all that air sent my tub shooting up into the sky!

"I went up, up, up, and I saw the world. It's so much prettier from above. You don't see the trash and the decay and the waste. And how lost so many people are. You see blue and green and blue and green. It's perfect from up there. Nothing out of place. Nothing forgotten. Everything flowing together perfectly, the way it was designed. No lonely bits or pieces that didn't fit. Everything just manages to belong.

"I could have stayed up there forever, but I was going to run out of hair spray eventually. So I used an old encyclopedia as an oar and I steered my tub, going to the brightest and biggest cluster of buildings I could see. Which was Chicago, of course. And I landed in Millennium Park. The boots on each foot of the tub cushioned the landing. Smoother than any seven-forty-seven.

"Problem was, when I left, my two daughters lived in the city. By the time I got back, they were gone. Suppose their mama took them away. I looked everywhere for them. Searched high and low. But I realized we traded places. I came home, and they went away. Maybe to the Land of Lost Things. So I guess Chicago wasn't really home. I tried looking for a home. Tried lots of different places. But none of them were where my daughters were. Until, finally, I found this here doughnut shop under the train tracks. And made myself a home of sorts. The next best thing. Lots of friends. My bottle caps. And all the doughnuts I could eat. Perfect pastry, really. One with a hole in it. For when there's a hole in your heart."

Without warning, I was reminded of something Violet once said to me: *Every person has some kind of story.*

I think all of us were reminded of that fact.

Violet's arms had fallen to her sides, Queenie's head upside down.

Michelle had a hand over her chest. Francis was pressed up against her shoulder.

TJ stood there with his mouth hanging open.

Morgan paused, wetting his chapped, cracked lips. And then looked up at me, his eyes cloudy. "How's that?" he asked.

"That's..." I couldn't find the words I wanted. Instead, I felt a wave of emotion breaking over me. It was too much. I didn't want to feel all that. I was afraid I was going to cry. I swallowed it back, as best I could. But my best didn't feel good enough, because the feeling lingered inside me.

"That's good, Morgan," I said, once I was sure my voice wouldn't break. "That's a great story. Really, really great."

Except that it wasn't a story at all. Not exactly.

He smiled, dipping his head. "Thanks, Cousin."

Violet cleared her throat. "We should...we should work on the knighting. That's what happens next, right?"

"Yeah," I said.

Michelle immediately jumped in with ideas, drawing

on the movies she'd seen about knights and crusades and courtly ladies. I tried to follow her, but out of the corner of my eye, I saw TJ. He was staring at Violet, with a sort of thoughtful expression on his face.

She noticed it, too.

"What is it?" Violet asked him, turning around and squatting down to his level.

"Do you think…" TJ trailed off, lost in some other world, his shoulder hunching up toward his ear.

"What, TJ?"

"You're really smart, Violet," he said.

She blinked in surprise. "Uh, thanks?"

"Do you think it's possible that other people also escaped from the Land of Lost Things, like Morgan?"

Violet shrugged. "I don't see why not," she said. "It's a world, not a prison, after all. Doors open both ways."

"So how come more people don't talk about it?"

"About what?"

"Escaping."

"Well," she said. "Maybe they don't think we'd believe them."

"Really?"

"Yeah."

He considered this for a moment. Slowly nodding to himself. "Yeah," he said. "That makes a lot of sense. And that makes it even more important."

"What?"

"Our charter."

"Telling people about the Land of Lost Things?"

"Yeah. Because, that way, once everyone knows, then everyone will believe it. And all the people who escaped, no one will be mad at them or anyone who sent them there."

Sent them there?

I wanted to ask what he meant by that, but Violet stopped me.

"Well, then," she said. "I guess that means we better get to work on this new video. How's it coming over there, Michelle? Leah?"

"We can do it just like they do it at the renaissance fair," Michelle said.

"You've been to the renaissance fair?" TJ asked.

"Of course!" she said. "Who doesn't go every summer?"

"We went twice last year," Violet said, looking a little grumpy about it. "My sister is obsessed. But, come on. We've got a job to do and a video to finish."

"Yeah!" TJ whooped.

I should have felt just as excited as the rest of them. But instead of soaring, I felt my heart sinking. Morgan's story was about a man who had failed in this world. A world that had failed him. That much I understood, even if I didn't know all the actual details of his life, all the steps along the path that had led him to the lonely little shop under the tracks. But where I was saddened by the story, TJ was excited.

Did he understand?

He was old enough to know that life wasn't fair.

I'd certainly known at his age.

I'd figured it out the day my dad left and I taught myself not to cry.

But something was wrong. And what bothered me more than the fact that something was wrong was the fact that I couldn't put a name to it.

Then TJ and Violet and Michelle were calling me over. We had a video to produce. And they couldn't do that without the camera.

That was my job.

I was in charge.

CHAPTER THIRTEEN

Well, only sort of in charge.

It didn't last that long.

Back in the apartment, I quickly learned who was *really* the boss.

"Leah." Aunt Lisa's expression was tight. "Your uncle and I need to talk to you. In our room, please."

Nothing good ever followed a sentence like that.

It was a couple of days after we filmed with Morgan. TJ and I had spent the entire morning with Violet and Michelle. Francis was in desperate need of repair, after his dryer-sheet feathers got caught on a strip of Velcro inside one of Michelle's bags. It was a surgical procedure. Accompanied by a story from Michelle. About how many lost cures and remedies made everyone in the Land of Lost Things well again.

No one died from disease.

It was truly an immortal land.

TJ really liked that part.

We came back home in time for dinner, but I noticed that Uncle Toby and Aunt Lisa kept cutting their eyes at each other. It wasn't their usual lovey-dovey googly eyes, either. And while Uncle Toby was as boisterous as ever, telling us about the dragon he'd slain at work—who would have guessed that being a mathematician was such a hazardous job?—Aunt Lisa was noticeably quiet.

Which usually meant she was thinking.

When I was helping clear the table, Aunt Lisa pulled me aside.

"Leah. Your uncle and I need to talk to you. In our room, please."

I felt an invisible hand start to squeeze my throat. I was pretty sure it was fear, but I didn't want to be afraid, so I tried to ignore it.

Uncle Toby and Aunt Lisa's room was at the very end of the long hallway of the apartment. They had a canopy bed, four high wooden posts with a gauzy white veil draped across the tops, drooping down in the middle like their own personal cloud. They sat me down on the foot of the bed. The two of them sat on a small love seat, on the opposite wall of the room, facing me. Uncle Toby had a bottle of orange pop in his hand, but Aunt Lisa didn't seem to care. She only had eyes for me, at the moment.

I somehow felt exactly the same way I had the last time I'd been sent to the principal's office.

"Leah," Uncle Toby said, leaning forward to plant his elbows on his knees. "We want to talk to you about—"

"About that video!" Aunt Lisa said.

Uncle Toby looked back at her. "Right. The video."

Oh no.

"Video?" I asked.

"Don't play dumb," Aunt Lisa said. "I always see right through that."

She really must have been a nightmare for her students.

"But—"

"HannahCantor777. I already spoke to your mother. She said that she never posted the video, but that you had her account password."

Right. I should have seen it coming. The video was posted under my mom's name, after all. Well. Both videos.

Wait.

There were *two* videos.

Which one were they talking about?

I cleared my throat gingerly. At the very least, I was sure I could wheedle that information out of Aunt Lisa, possibly without revealing that there were two, if she didn't

190

already know. I had to try, anyway. To see the bigger picture of exactly how much trouble I was in.

"Are you talking about the video with the…" I intentionally trailed off.

And she took the bait. "With Morgan, yes!" Aunt Lisa said.

I guess Violet was right. Everyone did know Morgan, after all.

But this wasn't good.

The video had turned out well. Really, really great, in fact. And by now, it was outpacing the first one. Leaving it in the dust, actually. I texted it to Nicole first, of course. She loved it immediately:

> Sending this to literally everyone I know right now!!

And she did. Again, it rippled through our friends to friends of our friends and on to their friends as well. Then, somewhere along the line, I guess someone showed it to their parents. All of a sudden, it was the parents who were passing it along instead. There was something about the puppets made of lost things, talking to a lost soul, that spoke to people. It was getting picked up and shared far beyond Deerwood Park now. Already, I'd caught wind of several Chicago celebs—the deputy mayor and the dean of Roosevelt University—sharing it out, saying it was some kind of lesson in compassion for vets. It wasn't what we'd meant to do. It didn't ever occur to me that Morgan even was a vet. Not until someone else said it. But Morgan's story had struck a chord. It was sending echoes into cyberspace.

And Morgan, of course, was a stranger.

Even if everyone knew him.

We'd broken every single rule of stranger danger.

And been caught in the act, by Aunt Lisa, a teacher, no less.

I should have figured it would come back to bite us.

I was already playing defense. "I know that it's not appropriate for us to be—"

"Tell me," Aunt Lisa interrupted, her voice getting a little shrill. "Who was Francis the flamingo?"

"Easy does it," Uncle Toby said to her, setting his bottle to one side. He took her hand between both of his and gave it a gentle squeeze.

"Uh." I blinked in surprise. I'd sort of expected the yelling to start now. "Uh, that was Michelle Green."

"Who?"

"Michelle Green. Her mom owns the laundromat on Frank Street."

"Oh!" Uncle Toby said. "Squeaky Green?"

"Yeah."

"I see," Aunt Lisa said, slipping her hand away from Uncle Toby. "And Queenie? Who was that?"

"Violet Kowalski."

"The girl from across the street," Uncle Toby said. "The one who lives in the parking space?"

I nodded.

Aunt Lisa rubbed her hands together. She set them on her knees. Then set them in her lap. She didn't seem to know what to do with them, so she folded them, interlacing her fingers. "And Staples?"

I heard a hitch in her breath.

And I knew I had to tell the truth.

"That's TJ," I said.

She took a sharp breath. And Uncle Toby put his arm around her waist, pulling her gently against his side. "TJ," she said, looking up at Uncle Toby.

A tear rolled down her face, leaving behind a mascara stain on her cheek.

Oh no. What had I done?

"I'm so sorry!" I blurted out, sliding off the bed and rushing over to them. I dropped to the floor in front of them, grabbing Aunt Lisa's hands. Begging for mercy felt like the best option. "I'm sorry. I know he shouldn't be talking to strangers. But we were making our video and—"

"You did it," Aunt Lisa said.

I stopped. I opened my mouth. Then shut it again. "Did it?"

"You got him to talk." She sniffled wetly. "He was talking!"

"Not just talking," said Uncle Toby. "He was making jokes. That was one funny hedgehog."

"How did you do it?" Aunt Lisa asked.

I looked back and forth between the two of them. In their eyes, I saw the same reaction that I'd had the night I followed TJ to Squeaky Green for the first time. The night I'd heard his little voice. I'd been caught completely off guard.

The only difference was that I'd had time, now, to get used to it.

Everything was completely new to them.

I should have said something before.

"I don't know," I said. And I really didn't. I guess I couldn't take credit for it. It was more Michelle's doing than mine. I'd just been nosy enough to be in the right place at the right time. Which was really more *Violet's* fault than mine.

"It's a miracle," Aunt Lisa said.

"You're not..." I paused. I had to swallow hard. "You're not angry?"

"Angry?" Uncle Toby said. He threw his head back and laughed. A full, rippling belly laugh that made the walls shake. "Why would we be angry?"

"You got our little boy talking," Aunt Lisa said. "Months with Ms. Weinstein haven't been able to make even the slightest difference." She broke off, swallowing back a sob.

Uncle Toby kissed the side of her head. "It's all right, *bubbeleh*. It's all right."

"Yes," Aunt Lisa said. "It's going to be."

Through the thin wall, we heard someone in the bathroom, running the sink. "That's TJ," Uncle Toby said. "Wait here a moment."

He stood up and ambled out of the room.

Aunt Lisa looked down at me, tears still shining in her eyes.

"You're really not mad at me?" I asked.

She let out a noise. Halfway between a laugh and a sob. And reached over to grab Uncle Toby's bottle, taking a big swig of pop before she put it back. "I was *furious* at first," she said. "Until I realized what was happening." She dragged the back of her hand across her eyes. She didn't realize that her mascara was running, and she smeared some of it across the bridge of her nose. She sniffled. "Let's just say you're getting a free pass. No one's getting grounded. *This* time. Just don't do something like *that* again."

"I promise," I said.

Uncle Toby came back in through the door, with a hand on TJ's shoulder, leading him inside. TJ shot me a look that I couldn't read, but I tried to offer him a reassuring smile. It was all right. Everything was going to be all right.

"Hello, sweetie," Aunt Lisa said, holding out her arms to him.

Hesitantly, he walked over and let her take his hands.

"TJ, I am *so proud* of you," she said, pulling him close and kissing each of his hands in turn.

Uncle Toby sat down on the couch again, putting his hand on the side of TJ's head. "We saw the video. It was really good."

"You were wonderful," Aunt Lisa said.

"Staples is my favorite character," Uncle Toby added.

"Mine, too."

TJ looked back and forth between the two of them.

"They're proud of you, Hedgehog," I said, trying to help.

But he still seemed blank.

"Tell me," Aunt Lisa said, kissing his temple. "Wherever did you come up with a story like that? It was so clever. I especially liked the part where—"

"It's not a story." TJ spoke. Except, it wasn't the TJ I'd spent the last couple of days with. It wasn't the laughing, charming boy with the puppet and the look of adoration in his eyes as he stared up at Michelle. This was the voice of a hollow boy. An angry boy. He was practically glaring at his mom.

From unseeing, colorless eyes.

Aunt Lisa blinked. "What?" she said. I felt like I could almost hear her dreams shattering, like a glass falling on the kitchen floor. This wasn't the TJ she'd been hoping for. The one she'd been trying so hard to get back.

"It's not a story," TJ said again.

"What do you mean, sweetie?"

"It's the truth," he said. "All of it. There *is* a Land of Lost Things."

"Of course," Uncle Toby said quickly. "We know that."

"Then why did you call it a story?"

Aunt Lisa and Uncle Toby looked at each other. Aunt Lisa tried to pull him close again, but TJ yanked his hands free, taking a step away from her. "TJ!"

"Say you were wrong," he said.

"What?"

"Say that it's not a story."

"It's not a story," Uncle Toby said.

TJ looked at his mom. Her eyes passed from Uncle Toby to me, back to Uncle Toby again. Finally, she settled her gaze on her son. She pulled herself up to her full height and squared her shoulders. "It's not a story," she said. Her voice struggled with each word. So this was what it sounded like when Aunt Lisa told a lie. "It's the truth."

I wouldn't say it made TJ happy. But he nodded. He seemed to accept that.

"But tell me," Aunt Lisa continued. Uncle Toby shot her a warning glance, but she kept going. "Where did you learn about the...Land of Lost Things?"

"I don't want to talk about it," TJ said.

"But we'd like to know—"

"I *said* I don't want to talk about it."

"Now, don't get upset with—"

"No!" TJ said.

With that, he whipped around and marched out of the room. Aunt Lisa tried to grasp at him, but he was too fast, and he closed the door behind him when she was only halfway there. I thought she might throw it open and chase after him, but she froze. And when we heard the door to his bedroom slam, she slowly turned to look at Uncle Toby.

He was there in a heartbeat, crossing to her in three strides and wrapping his arms around her. She buried her face in his shoulder and started to sob.

"Sh, sh, sh," he said, smoothing down her hair. "It's all right, *bubbeleh*. Small steps. That's what Ms. Weinstein said, remember? Small steps."

"Small steps," she said, her voice muffled by his shoulder.

"Baby steps."

"Baby steps."

"Our boy is talking," he continued. "That's a good step, right?"

"It's a good step."

"Right."

But if it was so good, why was it making Aunt Lisa cry like that?

I'd seen grown-ups cry before. In the movies. Professional actors who were paid to cry on cue and always managed to do it while still being glamorous. This was different somehow. Aunt Lisa looked so fragile, so small, wrapped up in Uncle Toby's arms. And Uncle Toby, well, he kind of looked like he wanted to cry, too. But he didn't. He wouldn't let himself. He just stood there, sturdy and proud and strong.

I guess he had to be the sturdy and proud and strong one.

Where would they be if both of them collapsed?

I needed to do something.

It was all my fault. The good and the bad of it. Probably the bad. Michelle was the only real force of good right now.

"I'll go talk to him," I said softly.

Uncle Toby looked at me. He tried to summon up the ghost of a smile. But it didn't quite reach his eyes, didn't flush his nose. "Thank you, Leah."

I didn't want to be thanked.

Not when I hadn't done anything worth thanking.

But I gave him a little nod. "It's . . . it's going to be okay. It's just. I don't know." And I quietly slipped out of the room, turning the doorknob so that it wouldn't click or snap when I closed the door.

I'm not sure it really mattered, though.

Aunt Lisa wouldn't have heard it.

The second I was out of the room, I think something inside her broke. She started crying in a big way, sobbing so loudly that I could hear her through the door. Uncle Toby was muttering something under his breath, comforting words, I guess. I couldn't tell exactly what he was saying, but I understood the way he was saying it. It didn't seem to work.

Her crying just got louder and louder.

I felt tears start stinging the backs of my eyes.

Was I about to cry?

No. No, I didn't cry. That wasn't me.

I refused.

Swallowing hard, I turned to face the stretch of hall in front of me.

CHAPTER FOURTEEN

Even though I knocked, I didn't wait for TJ to tell me that I could come in. I just opened the door. He was sitting on his bed, in the same position where he spent most of my first few days in the apartment. It was so startling to see him back that way that I heard my mom's voice in my ear all over again:

He isn't talking.

But unlike a week ago, he actually turned and looked at me. His eyes landed on me. And I knew for sure that he saw me there.

Yes.

He was talking.

And I wouldn't forget it.

I wasn't quite sure what to say, though, because I still didn't really understand what had happened, why he'd blown up the way he had.

But I knew that the last thing I wanted to do was repeat Aunt Lisa's mistakes.

So I started by taking a seat on his bed. Leaving a lot of room between us. We weren't touching, and I wasn't crowding him.

So he didn't squirm and try to escape.

For a little while, we sat there quietly. I tried to strain, to hear Aunt Lisa crying, but she was too far away. It didn't matter if I could hear it for real or not. I still heard it inside my head.

Poor Aunt Lisa.

The air-conditioning unit kicked on, and the curtains blew, billowing into the room. TJ and I both turned to watch them dance for a while.

I was the one who finally broke the silence. "Hey," I said to him.

Maybe it wasn't the most original conversation starter, but it seemed to do the trick.

"Hey," TJ said back.

Carefully, I scooted a little closer to him on the bed. Still not touching. But we were in each other's space now, a little bit.

He didn't pull away.

I waited again. Partly to let him adjust to the new circumstances. And partly because I was still trying to figure out what to say. "Do you want to talk about it?" I finally asked.

"Not really," he said.

"Okay," I said.

TJ was the champion of sitting in silence.

I definitely wasn't.

I tried to wait it out as long as I could, but that wasn't very long at all. "Can I ask you something?"

"I guess," he replied.

"It's about Michelle."

He turned to look at me.

"I'm just wondering..." My tongue felt heavy and clumsy. "Well, this is going to sound kind of weird."

"What?"

"Do you not like sharing her?"

"Sharing her?"

"With Violet and me."

He shrugged.

"It's just that you got very upset with your parents when they called the Land of Lost Things a 'story.'"

"It's *not* a story!"

"I know!" I said quickly, holding up both hands. I didn't actually know, but I knew what I needed to do to continue the conversation. "I know."

He narrowed his eyes at me, but didn't look away.

"What I mean is: the Land of Lost Things means a lot to you."

"Yeah."

"And I'm wondering if you would be happier keeping it between Michelle and you, instead of sharing it with everyone."

"Our club's charter—"

"Is to share it," I said. "I know that."

"We have to share it."

"But it's making you unhappy." I dared to reach out, to put a hand on his shoulder. "I don't have to keep posting the videos, Hedgehog."

"I don't care about the videos," he said, looking down, off to the side.

That hurt. Unexpectedly so.

I realized in that moment that even if he didn't care about the videos, I did. I looked forward to working on them so much. We'd already filmed our third and were planning out the fourth. Each time, I thought, I was getting a little better at it. And it wasn't like school. I could practice multiplication and fractions every day. It was just automatic. A formula. With the videos, I felt like I was really *doing* something. Building something.

But it wasn't about me.

Even if it hurt a little.

"Okay." I kept my hand where it was. "What do you care about?"

"I just want to keep doing what we're doing. I want to keep visiting Michelle and Squeaky Green."

"We can do that."

"I want to learn everything I can about the Land of Lost Things."

"Everything you can?"

"Everything Michelle knows," he said. "And you and Violet," he added, as an afterthought.

"Of course."

"That's what matters," he said.

But that wasn't what mattered. Not all of it, anyway. There was so much more to his unhappiness. I could almost reach out and touch it. Except that I couldn't. It slipped away, out of my grasp.

Uncle Toby and Aunt Lisa kept thanking me, but they shouldn't have thanked me at all. I didn't know what I was doing.

Suddenly, I wanted to throw myself into Uncle Toby's arms and sob.

Which was ridiculous.

TJ scooted a little closer to me. To my surprise, he lay down, resting his head on my knee. We used to sit like this all the time. Every summer before, after our adventures and photos. "Leah?" he said.

"Yeah, Hedgehog?"

"Will you tell me a story? Like you used to."

"Sure," I said. I looked over at his shelves of books. "What do you want?"

"No. Not one of *those* stories. A real one. Will you tell me more about the Land of Lost Things?"

"I..."

"Please?"

I touched the curls falling against the side of his face. They were so soft. Gently, I leaned over and kissed his temple. "Okay," I said. I'm pretty sure I would have said yes to anything if only to keep us this way a little while longer. "What do you want to hear?"

"I want to hear about the people there."

"The people?"

"Yeah."

"Well." Oh boy. "You already know about Amelia Earhart."

"The aviator."

"Good memory, Hedgehog. Actually, I was reading about her last night," I said. I slipped my phone out of my pocket and opened the browser. The Wikipedia page was still open, but I had to click back and back and back (from volcanic islands to American Samoa to Spanish flu) until I returned to Amelia and her black-and-white picture smiling at me.

"Here, take a look." I turned the phone so he could see. "It says here that she had an endorsement deal for luggage. I guess this was before luggage got lost at airports all the time, huh?"

TJ barely even glanced at the picture. "Who else?" he asked.

"Who else?"

"Yeah. Besides her. Who else lives in the Land of Lost Things?"

"Well, let me see." I thumbed down to the bottom of the page. There was a link to a category called "1930s missing person cases" and I tapped it. I was hoping for a bit of inspiration, but I was surprised by the huge list of names. A lot of people disappeared. A lot of people were lost.

How did that even happen?

At the bottom of the page, I clicked "missing person cases by decade." It went back centuries. How could I even pick one?

I clicked "1590s missing person cases" at random and picked the first one that looked interesting.

"Virginia Dare," I said.

There was something familiar about the name, but I couldn't place it.

"Who's that?" TJ asked.

I scanned the new page, and started to remember

something about this from a social studies class. "Have you ever heard of the colony of Roanoke?" I asked.

"No."

"It was one of the first English colonies in the country."

"So?"

"So, a group of settlers came to the colony. Men and women and even kids. Including a baby named Virginia Dare. But then, nobody knows how or why, the whole colony just disappeared."

"The whole colony?"

"The man who founded it went off to England for a little while, and when he came back, it was just gone."

"All of them?"

"One day it was there. The next it was gone. No sign of any of the people. They were never heard from again. Look, here. There's a picture." Sort of. "They put Virginia Dare and her family on a stamp, see?"

I turned the picture for him to see, but TJ batted my hand away. "They disappeared because they went to the Land of Lost Things?"

"Makes sense, doesn't it?"

"Yeah."

"Virginia Dare was very famous for a while," I said.

"Who else?"

"Who else?"

"Yes. Who else lives in the Land of Lost Things?"

Everyone else on the "1590s missing person cases" page was connected to Virginia Dare, I figured, since their last names were all "Dare," so I went back to the page on "missing person cases by decade" and picked the 1970s. There were a lot of names to choose from. "Well," I said, settling on the first name I saw. "There was Juanita Nielsen...."

"Who's she?"

I loaded the page. "She was a famous journalist who—"

"I don't want to hear about more *famous* people," TJ said.

I looked down at him. "What do you mean?"

"Amelia Earhart," he said, "was famous, and Virginia Dare was famous, and this journalist was famous."

"Yeah."

"But what about normal people?"

"Normal people?"

"Yeah. Just normal people. Regular people. Famous people aren't the only ones who get lost," he said.

"I guess."

"Morgan isn't famous."

"No, not really." Except for the part where he was becoming a local internet sensation. But I didn't want to talk about the videos right now.

"There must be a lot more people in the Land of Lost Things than just famous people," TJ said.

"Of course there are," I said.

"Then why don't you tell me about them?"

"Well..." I wasn't nearly as good at this without Michelle and Violet. "We talk about the famous people in the Land of Lost Things just because of that. Because they *are* famous. Because we've heard of them."

"But what about the normal people?"

"Think about it," I said. "If I knew about the normal people, wouldn't that make them famous people, instead of normal?"

TJ frowned a little. I could see him trying to weigh the thought out. I held my breath until he finally nodded. "I guess that makes sense."

I was so glad it did.

What else could I say?

"But there *are* normal people there, right?" he asked.

"Of course. There are more normal people than famous people everywhere. Plenty of people in the Land of Lost Things are just as unspecial as me."

"You're special," TJ said.

What?

I stared at him for a long moment. TJ wasn't looking at me. I wondered if he understood what he was saying. What "special" actually meant. "You think so?"

He nodded against my leg. I wanted to ask him more, to ask him why he thought that when I didn't even believe it about myself, but he kept going. "And kids, too. Lots of kids in the Land of Lost Things, right?"

"Well, not a lot of kids get lost, I hope."

"But some do?"

I nodded. "Some do. Like Peter Pan. You know? Peter Pan and the Lost Boys. I'll bet they're there."

"I think so," TJ said. "But they're famous."

"Right."

"And they're not normal."

"No," I said. "I guess not." What with the flying and the fighting pirates and all.

"There are other boys there, too."

It wasn't a question.

TJ's breathing was starting to get heavy. He pulled his knees up against his chest. And only moments after that, he fell asleep, right on top of me. The wrinkles in his forehead smoothed out. He was my little Hedgehog, curled up against me.

If only he could always look this peaceful.

I waited for a while. Maybe half an hour or so. And then, very carefully, I slid out from under him, slipping a pillow in my place. He let out a soft grunt but didn't wake up. I pulled a sheet over him, even though he was sleeping facing the wrong way. With a kiss on his head, I left him in his room and crossed the hall.

The hallway was empty. And the living room, too. The door to Uncle Toby and Aunt Lisa's room was still shut.

I closed my own door and sat down on the sleeper sofa.

And I started to cry.

The problem was, I didn't know why.

CHAPTER FIFTEEN

No one talked about what happened.

Aunt Lisa stuck to the weather and the crafts fair.

Uncle Toby told more CIA and saber-toothed tiger stories.

I wasn't about to let it slip that I'd broken a four-year record of not crying.

And TJ? Well, TJ didn't say anything at all. Except when we were in Squeaky Green, of course. So we kept going back. Day after day. How could we not? I needed to hear his voice. And for some reason, TJ needed Squeaky Green.

Michelle started making dresses for Queenie. Royal gowns out of old scarves and fabric hats, modeled off pictures from her social studies textbook. They were in shades of blue and purple. Always trimmed in some kind of precious metal, made out of broken necklace chains and bracelets from the lost and found. Eventually, I decided we should do a series of fashion shoots for Queenie, including a video of her walking down the catwalk. Or, rather, buzzing down the catwalk. Beewalk? Something like that, anyway. I spent several nights watching fashion show clips—mostly to keep myself from crying again—so I knew all the right moves to teach Violet. Francis gave a running commentary, discussing each gown's designer, usually a famous historical figure, like Cleopatra or Billie Holiday. And Staples served as the very enthusiastic audience.

The next video had Staples and Francis engaged in a joust, using lances made out of rolled-up newspapers, tightly bound together with cut wristbands from water parks and clubs in the area. I looked up the rules online. Staples, of course, won every bout (that's what you call a round in jousting). He was *Sir* Staples, after all. He couldn't very well lose. But Francis found increasingly hilarious and ridiculous ways to excuse his poor performance. Everything from hangnails to the dog eating his jousting homework. Queen Queenie awarded Staples with a handkerchief, as a favor and token of her appreciation. Michelle said that's how they did things back in the olden days. He was declared Sir Staples the Brave, the bravest of the brave, at TJ's request.

The video after that was devoted to the secret tunnel entrance to the Land of Lost Things, in one of Squeaky Green's dryers.

We had to film that one early in the morning, before any customers stopped by to do their laundry.

"All right," I said, sitting on top of one of the washing machines to line up the shot. "Puppets up."

Violet, TJ, and Michelle were all lying on their backs in front of the open door to dryer number five. In unison, they raised their arms and the puppets appeared on-screen.

"Great," I said. "Just great. Queenie, move in a little closer."

"You're being very picky about the shots, Leah," Violet said.

"It has to be perfect."

"If I move in much closer, I'm going to be lying on top of them," she replied. But she still managed to maneuver her arm a little bit closer. Without lying on top of TJ and Michelle, thankfully.

I adjusted the angle of the phone, careful to cut out any hint of Violet's slender wrist, the bracelets that had fallen around Michelle's elbow, TJ's wrinkled blue sleeve. "Let's run through the opening," I said.

"We *know* the opening," Violet whined.

"Fine. How about the middle, then? The story about the entrance?"

"Better."

"Start us off, Leah," TJ said. "But only for pretend. Like we're doing it for real, but not yet. Rehearsing."

"Okay," I said. "Lights! Camera! Action!"

The characters came to life on the screen.

"Today, we're going to show you one of the secret entrances to the Land of Lost Things," Queenie said.

"There are so many secret entrances out there," Francis said. "But this is one of our favorites."

"It's in Squeaky Green Coin-Op Laundromat," Staples said. There was no sense in hiding where we were. The world had already seen. And seemed to like knowing that there were adventures to be had in Oak Lake.

Queenie nodded her head, which was really most of her body. "That's right, Sir Staples the Brave. Dozens of people walk past this entrance every day, and they don't even know it's there."

"But that's life," Francis said. "So many people never notice what's right in front of them."

"Which is really kind of sad, when you think about it," Staples said.

I hadn't really thought about it. Not while we were coming up with what each of the characters would say. But something about the way TJ spoke through Sir Staples made me feel a sort of pang of emotion I hadn't expected. I had no name for it. Other than a sort of rush of truth.

My eyes started to sting. But I blinked them hard. I had to keep paying attention.

"The entrance to my Land of Lost Things is in the most ordinary of places," Queenie said.

"It's a dryer!" Staples said.

Francis turned his beak to the camera. "Have you ever noticed that sometimes a sock disappears after being tumbled dry? Maybe you thought it just got caught somewhere or dropped or misplaced. But today you're going to learn the truth. And the truth is simply that the sock slipped through a secret portal to the Land of Lost Things, a portal right here in the back of the dryer!"

"It's not the only entrance, of course," Queenie said. "There are lots of entrances, all over the planet."

"But this is the busiest!"

"And now you know the truth," Staples said.

"So the next time you lose a sock after laundry day," Francis said, "don't blame your mommy or daddy."

"Just know that your sock has come to reside in my kingdom." Queenie buzzed with pride. "And that it's in good hands."

Michelle let out a peal of laughter. One that definitely wasn't planned.

"Michelle!" TJ said, sitting up.

"What was that?" Violet asked, propping herself up on her elbow.

I dropped my arms.

"Sorry, sorry." Michelle wiped her eyes with her free hand, scooting herself up against the bank of dryers. "It's just that it was funny."

"What?"

"Good hands." She waved Francis, wiggling her fingers in his beak. "And our *hands* are in the socks right now."

Violet raised both eyebrows.

"Quit messing around," TJ said. "This is important."

"Sorry, TJ." She shook her head. "I was just thinking. What if someone's missing sock was on-screen right now? Maybe someone was looking at Francis and going, 'Hey, that's mine!'"

"'Those kids are thieves!'" Violet said.

"That won't happen," TJ replied. "We aren't thieves. The other socks are in the Land of Lost Things."

"Of course, of course."

He gave Violet a stern look, before turning to me. "Let's start again from the beginning. Give us a 'Lights! Camera! Action!'"

"Okay, Hedgehog," I said, shaking out my arms before I raised the camera to frame them again.

The three of them neatly arranged themselves on the floor.

"Lights! Camera! Action!"

CHAPTER SIXTEEN

By the last week of my visit in Chicago, HannahCantor777 had gained a lot more attention. When we began posting, my mom's account had only five followers. Two professors she was friends with and three cousins, who lived in New York City. But with each video, the following went up. It wasn't just people we knew anymore. Now strangers were hopping on, eager to see the next Land of Lost Things video.

Our videos got lots of comments. Of course, there were plenty of trolls out there, making fun of our "cheap" puppets and lousy video quality. I'm not going to lie, that kind of stung a little. Maybe a lot. I was feeling kind of raw after

I had my cry. But, seriously, what were they expecting? A three-camera setup with puppets fresh from the Jim Henson workshop? We were just students, after all.

Still, most of the feedback we got was pretty great.

> I love all three characters! Will there be any more?

> Thank you for helping us remember that there are lost people among us. It's important we pay attention so they don't end up in the Land of Lost Things again. <3

> Francis is so funny!

> You go, Oak Lake! Represent!

> Where did you come up with such an amazing story?

That last one upset TJ.

"It's not a story!" he said.

"I know, Hedgehog," I said, rubbing his shoulder.

"It's not!"

I decided after that to be more careful when I showed the others all the comments we were getting.

But we saw the Land of Lost Things taking off in other ways.

After we posted the dryer episode, Michelle's mom

came to us to thank us for mentioning Squeaky Green. Business was picking up.

We saw it, too.

Since our faces were never on-screen, we could walk anonymously through the laundromat, watching as strangers slipped inside, taking pictures of dryer number five, where we'd been filming.

The regulars griped a little bit:

"All these people wandering around. It's hard to get work done."

"I have to wait ten minutes to get a washer!"

"Who are all these people?"

But Michelle's mom was so happy she even put a sign out in front, announcing Squeaky Green had been a filming location for several Land of Lost Things stories.

"They're not *stories*!" TJ said.

It was such a sore point that Michelle got her mom to change the wording on the sign from "stories" to "videos."

Maybe the most amazing part of it all, though, was what we saw happening with Morgan. We'd promised Uncle Toby and Aunt Lisa again and again that we wouldn't film with him anymore. But what was already out in the world was out in the world. And we still walked the same route to and from Squeaky Green every day.

Now, when we passed under the tracks, we'd spot people who'd just gotten off the train, flocking to Morgan's little shop. Sometimes, they'd ask him if they could take a picture with him. He always said no. But they also bought boxes and boxes of doughnuts. And some of them asked about his missing daughters: What were their names? How old were they? Did he think they could have seen the video? It was more attention than I'd ever seen him receive, and I was glad for it. His life had seemed so silent and hopeless before, sitting alone in his shop with nothing to talk about except doughnuts. But now he had company.

Life was changing for everyone and everything that our videos touched.

Except for TJ.

TJ was the same.

Wednesday night, I walked into the bathroom to brush my teeth before bed.

I was trapped in the sorrow
Surrendered to despair
Went looking for myself
But couldn't find "me" anywhere

I was singing softly, so the upstairs neighbors wouldn't start beating on the ceiling, demanding that we turn off the garbage disposal, which is, I was sure, exactly what my voice sounded like. I would absolutely never admit it to Violet, but I was starting to really get into Dina and the Starlights.

Finally wrote my own story
And I found my own sound
Learned you can't really lose
What was meant to be found

I opened my mouth to start the next verse, but instead, a tuneless "Gah!" escaped my throat, when I looked in the mirror. I spun around. Behind me was the bathtub, and the curtain was drawn back at the moment. TJ was sitting in the tub. It was empty, and he was wearing his Kermit the Frog pj's, covered in googly eyes, rainbows, and little banjos.

Just sitting there.

His arms around his knees.

It had been a hard day. Instead of going to Squeaky Green with me, he had to go to Ms. Weinstein's office with Aunt Lisa. Both of them returned tight-lipped and unhappy. And each disappeared into their own room. Neither one came out again until Uncle Toby got home, carrying two heavy bags of takeout. Dinner was both of them staring down at their plates of broccoli chicken while Uncle Toby made up a bizarre story about how he invented a time machine to travel back to ancient China to get our food.

His version of the CIA was truly capable of anything.

Of course, TJ hadn't said a word the whole meal. But something told me that he was ready to talk now.

"What are you doing, Hedgehog?" I asked breathlessly, walking over to the ledge of the tub and perching near him.

"I was just thinking," he said, in a faraway kind of voice.

"Thinking about what?"

"About how I could turn the tub into a flying machine."

"Like Morgan?"

He nodded.

"Why would you want to do that?"

"Well," he said, "I figure that if Morgan could use it to fly back from the Land of Lost Things, maybe I could use it to fly there."

"I think you'd need a lot of hair spray."

"Mommy uses a lot," he said.

I had to stifle a laugh. Aunt Lisa used more hair spray than anyone I knew. First thing in the morning, she always seemed to carry a cloud of it with her to the breakfast table. Over the day, it would diffuse a little bit. But even in a stiff wind, her hair never seemed to move all that much.

"True," I said, swinging my legs over the ledge, so I could fall down in the tub beside TJ. I pulled him up against my side. He let me hold him. "And what would you use to steer?"

"Morgan used an old encyclopedia."

"We don't have any encyclopedias. Only Wikipedias."

TJ shrugged. "I'm sure any book would work."

"Maybe."

"And we have a lot of them."

"Oh, but it would be way too scary," I said.

"Sir Staples is Sir Staples the Brave. I can be, too."

"Can be what?"

"Brave."

"Of course."

I leaned my head against his, his soft curls tickling my cheek. We sat there quietly for a moment. I was still missing part of the story. TJ seemed so unhappy. In spite of the fact that things were amazing right now.

He let out a long sigh.

"What is it, Hedgehog?" I asked. "What's wrong?"

"It's just..."

"Tell me."

"I keep asking Michelle when we can actually *go* to the Land of Lost Things," he said. "Instead of just talking about it."

Almost every day now, in fact. We could never really leave Squeaky Green without the question coming up.

"And she keeps saying the same thing, over and over and over again."

" 'Soon,' " I said.

"Soon." He pulled away from me, turning his face up to look me in the eye. "When is 'soon' going to happen?"

"I don't know, Hedgehog."

"Is it going to happen?"

I stared at him. Long and hard. And wondered how to answer. What was I supposed to tell him? No, of course "soon" wasn't going to happen. There was no Land of Lost Things. Not really. It was just a story. But any time someone used the word "story," he got so upset.

Did he not understand?

It wasn't the first time I'd wondered.

It *was* just a story.

TJ had to know that, deep down. He was a smart kid. He'd grown up understanding that any time Uncle Toby started talking about the CIA or other planets or dragons, the only response was to groan and roll your eyes. And Aunt Lisa. She'd read to him every night since he was little. His room was filled with picture books. When she started insisting he write a hundred words a day, he even wrote his own fairy tales.

He was literally surrounded by stories.

He had to know what one was, when he saw it.

"Leah?" he asked.

I realized I'd gone silent. My nose had that funny, tickly feeling that came with tears. Once I'd allowed myself to cry, it was harder to control than before.

I had changed.

"When are we going to go to the Land of Lost Things?"

Never.

But looking down at his little face, intense and full of hope.

How could I say that to him?

I was beginning to understand why Michelle always used the word "soon." It was an easier answer.

Easier than the truth.

"I don't know," I said.

It wasn't "soon." But all the same, TJ accepted it. Not happily. But willingly. He nodded a little and settled against my side again. "I hope it's soon-soon," he said.

"Me too, Hedgehog."

I hoped it was soon. I hoped it was always "soon." Because any other answer and I didn't know what would happen.

But it scared me.

I was just getting my cousin back. The Land of Lost Things was bringing him back from being lost.

I didn't want to lose him again.

And I saw now how very easy that might be.

After everyone was asleep that night, I made a decision. As quietly as possible, I opened the study door and crept into the hallway, trying to avoid the creakiest of floorboards, as

I tiptoed into the front room. Beyond the table, with all of Aunt Lisa's plans for the fair, was the cabinet, where she'd hidden away her binder and the book. I'd been thinking about it, off and on, for what felt like forever. Now I knew I needed to see what she was hiding.

If she caught me, I would be in *so much* trouble.

But it had to be worth it.

I opened one of the cabinet doors and found the book, *Psychological Trauma and Recovery*, right on top. The binder was beside it. When I pulled it out, it seemed thicker than before. Like she'd been adding more lists.

I sat down on the floor and opened it to the first page. "Children with acute stress reactions," it read on top, followed by a thick block of text, filled with words that I couldn't even begin to understand. "Hypoperfusion"? "PTSD"? What were those? I jabbed my finger at one of them, as if it were a link that would magically open to a new page with a definition. But paper didn't work that way. You had to read it in a straight line, without taking side trips to new pages. I gave up on scanning the page after a minute, turning to the next one. "Healing after a school shooting," it read. And more blocks of text. I decided to read it out loud, under my breath, to force myself to understand it.

"Fear, rage, anxiety, detachment, depression, and difficulty sleeping are just a few of the symptoms associated with the months following an acute trauma, such as surviving a school shooting."

Fear? Well, TJ did flinch at loud noises.

Rage? I still couldn't explain how he got so angry at his parents.

Anxiety? I wasn't sure about that one. But I thought about him sitting in the bathtub. There was something anxious about him.

I kept flipping through the pages, reading them as best I could, but I started to see more of the same things, over and over again.

Psychological damage.

Trauma.

Symptoms.

Survivor's guilt.

Stimuli.

Social anxiety.

Isolation.

Selective mutism.

I got back to the lists, offering suggestions of how to help kids after a school shooting: listen, be reassuring, make them feel safe, don't let them watch the news, promise them the world is really a good place, give them healthy food, take care of yourself.

Be there for them.

Show empathy.

I knew that word: "empathy." It meant feeling what someone else was feeling.

Something I guess I wasn't too good at doing, considering the way I always bottled up my emotions. You couldn't feel what someone else was feeling when you didn't allow yourself to feel anything at all.

Except that something inside me had shifted, when I let myself cry for the first time in four years. I was different now. A door had opened.

I was sad, I realized, because TJ was sad.

I really could feel what he was feeling.

But empathy wasn't enough. I still didn't have the answers. I didn't know why he was sad. And I didn't know how to cure that sadness, either.

None of the suggestions in the binder felt like what he really wanted.

I knew what he wanted. He wanted to go to the Land of Lost Things. But how could I help TJ when the one thing he wanted was just impossible?

CHAPTER SEVENTEEN

The back room of the laundromat had become a sort of clubhouse. It was a sacred space for the members of the Lost Things Club to hang out, even when we weren't making a new video. Michelle's talent for finding lost things provided endless hours of entertainment. When Violet, TJ, and I arrived every morning, she'd have her latest finds from the evening washing shift. She would lay them out on the table. Some of them would be used for our puppets, who suffered wear and tear with each new video. But others would just leave us incredibly confused.

"What *is* it?" Violet asked on Thursday morning, picking up an object Michelle had discovered wedged in the corner of one of the washing machines. Machine number fifteen, which always provided us with the most treasures. We were each sitting in one of the chairs around the table.

Michelle in the squashy chair.

TJ in the wooden chair with the cracked leather seat.

Violet in the black plastic chair.

And me in the folding chair.

We hadn't exactly, *officially* declared each seat as our own. But we all just sort of gravitated to them.

Michelle's latest find was about two inches long and made of glossy black plastic. It was shaped like a rectangle, with the corners slightly rounded. One side had a raised edge going all around the border. Like the lip of a bowl. On the other side, there were two prongs, slightly sticky, standing out from the otherwise smooth surface.

"I'm not sure," Michelle said, as Violet passed it over to her. She examined it a moment, then passed it to TJ.

TJ flipped it over and over in his hands, then held it out to me. I realized a second too late that I was staring at him. A hard, intense look. After everything I'd read in the binder and book, I felt like I was seeing him in new ways. Searching him.

Look for symptoms of trauma, all the articles and lists said.

Was he shifting in his chair because he was anxious?

Or because the cracked seat was poking him?

How could you tell the difference?

Was his shoulder hunched up because he was tense?

Or was that what he looked like when he was relaxed?

I didn't know anymore.

I was questioning everything.

"Leah?" he asked, wrinkling his nose.

"Nothing!" I blurted out. Before I realized he hadn't asked me a question.

I felt the three of them staring at *me* for a second.

"Okay, then," Violet said, raising both eyebrows.

"Maybe it's some kind of button?" Michelle said, gesturing to the piece of black plastic, sitting in the sweaty palm of TJ's hand.

"No," I said, taking it from him. "No holes. I think it's completely solid." But I gripped both of the shorter ends and, on instinct, gave it a pull. To my surprise, it slid open.

"Oh!" I said. "I know what it is!"

"What?" Violet asked.

"It's a . . . I don't know if there's a word for it."

"That's helpful."

"You stick it on your laptop, over the webcam," I said. "And then you can slide it open when you need to use the camera, then shut it when you're done so if a hacker turns on your camera, they won't be able to see anything."

"How'd that end up in the washer?"

"Must have been in someone's pocket," Michelle said.

Violet shook her head. "I'll never understand people.

You check your pockets before you do laundry. Isn't that obvious?"

"Not to everyone."

Violet sighed. "People need to take better care of their stuff."

TJ nodded silently in agreement.

There was a sudden knock on the door. TJ flinched.

I wondered if he was reliving the noise of the bullets going off in the school.

Like the car backfiring.

Like the car door slamming shut.

Aunt Lisa's papers talked about that.

"Who's that?" Violet asked. "Is that your mother?"

Michelle rolled her eyes. "My mama has a key. It's her coin-op."

Violet scowled. "Can we just pretend I didn't ask that?"

"Nope," Michelle said. "I'm going to remember it for the rest of my life." She hopped up and trotted over to the door. After pulling it open a crack to peer outside, she pulled it open the rest of the way.

On the other side was Aunt Lisa.

Seeing her in the laundromat felt all wrong. Like when you changed the channels too fast and the shows you were seeing kind of blurred into one another. She just didn't fit in. Didn't belong in this world. Didn't belong with the rest of the scenery.

"Hello, all," she said, with a brittle, forced smile that anyone could tell was, well, not fake, but not exactly coming from a happy place, either. "I'm TJ's mother. Lisa Whitman-Cantor. I hope I'm not interrupting anything. I know you creative types have your process. I don't want to get in the way of that."

"Nope," Michelle said, stepping off to one side and raising one leg, balancing on the other. "Come on in."

Aunt Lisa breezed inside, carrying a tray covered in aluminum foil. "I thought you filmmakers might get a little hungry, so I brought you a snack."

Violet cleared a space on the table for Aunt Lisa to set down the tray, shoving aside a pile of mismatched socks. "This is a secret family recipe," she said, taking off the foil to reveal a platter piled high with apple-cinnamon sticky buns.

"They look amazing!" Michelle said.

I could already feel my mouth watering. They were my absolute favorite. Aunt Lisa made them every Thanksgiving, when she came up to Deerwood Park with the family.

They weren't exactly a health food.

Maybe she'd given up on that particular list.

Couldn't blame her. I still didn't see how healthy food was supposed to get through to TJ.

"Dig in, kids," she said, smiling at us.

"Thanks!" Violet said.

"Yeah," Michelle added. "Thank you so much."

TJ came around the table to take a sticky bun. His movements were hesitant, halting. Like he was afraid Aunt Lisa was going to grab him or something.

"Thank you, Mommy."

It was the first time he'd spoken to her since their blowup in her room. My eyes cut over to Aunt Lisa. She very, very quickly dragged her hand across her eyes, turning just slightly so TJ couldn't see.

Fortunately, she had her waterproof mascara on today.

We helped ourselves to the treats. They were just as buttery rich as I remembered, and I practically inhaled the first one before reaching for a second.

Aunt Lisa once claimed that the recipe was the only thing her mom ever gave her.

It seemed like a pretty great secret to receive.

"Oh, these are soooooooo gooooooood," Violet said.

"You eat as many as you like," Aunt Lisa said. "We need to put some meat on your bones. And, while I have you all here," she continued, "there's something I want to ask you. Something I hope you'll consider."

"What?" Michelle asked.

"Well, it's about the crafts fair."

"Crafts fair?"

"The Oak Lake crafts fair. It's coming up this weekend."

"You're on the planning committee for that, aren't you?" Violet asked.

It figured Violet would know.

"Yes," Aunt Lisa said. "And it seems we have an empty booth that needs filling. One of our artists had to cancel at the last minute. I was wondering if the four of you would be interested in using the booth."

Violet lofted both eyebrows. "We don't really have any crafts to sell," she said.

"Oh, I know, I know." Aunt Lisa smiled at her. "I wasn't thinking about you using the booth to sell. I was actually wondering if you'd like to use the booth to put on some puppet shows."

Michelle's eyes lit up. "Really?"

"Your Land of Lost Things videos are so popular," Aunt Lisa said. "I thought we might take advantage of that a little bit. There will be a lot of kids coming to the fair with their parents. And I'm sure they'll get bored, just walking through the rows. I think it would be fun for them to set up by your booth and watch some shows."

I noticed that she was careful not to use the word "stories."

It was "videos."

It was "shows."

She'd figured out that "stories" was... what had the binder said? A trigger word?

Yes, that was it.

A trigger word. A word that inspires someone to act a certain way. Or, in TJ's case, react.

It seemed like a cruel figure of speech to use, when talking about someone who had survived a school shooting.

And apparently, everyone developed different trigger words. None of the articles suggested that "stories" would be one. But we'd seen firsthand how TJ reacted.

Aunt Lisa knew that. Didn't she?

"That could be a lot of fun!" Michelle said.

Violet nodded. "And we could film a promo for the crafts fair today."

"Yeah!"

"That would be wonderful," Aunt Lisa said.

"Well, I'm down for it," Michelle said.

"Me too," Violet replied.

I raised my hand. "Me three."

We all turned to look at TJ.

And immediately felt a sense of disappointment.

TJ was frowning. In fact, he was downright scowling. His eyes flicked back and forth, among the three of us. "I don't know," he said, hunching his shoulder.

"Why not?" Violet asked.

"There will be a lot of people."

"So?"

"Remember our charter, TJ?" Michelle said. "We need to spread the word to as many people as we can."

"But this isn't on video. This is in front of people." He set down his sticky bun, appetite suddenly gone.

"You don't need to be shy, TJ."

"Yeah," Violet said. "We'll be hidden from sight. That's how puppet shows work."

Violet and Michelle were so excited. And TJ just wasn't buying it.

"We can build a barrier," I said, trying to find a way to make it work for everyone. "Something that has 'Land of Lost Things' on the front." I swept my arm through the air, trying to make him see it. "You'll be hiding behind it the whole time."

TJ looked at me, his expression softening a little bit. "No one will see us?"

"No," I said. "Only the puppets."

He nodded. Just slightly.

I was doing better with this empathy thing. I'd picked up on his fear and found a way to soothe it.

"Well," Violet said, clapping her hands together. "There's an easy way to settle this. We are part of a club, after all."

"What's that?" Michelle asked.

"We put it to a simple vote. All those in favor of performing at the Oak Lake crafts fair, raise your hand."

Violet's hand went up.

Michelle's shot up, too.

I raised my hand cautiously.

And as we watched, TJ very, very slowly raised his hand.

"Okay," Violet said. "That settles it. It's unanimous. The motion passes."

"So you'll do it?" Aunt Lisa asked.

"We'll do it."

"Oh! Wonderful!" She reached out, touching each of us one by one on top of the head. "Thank you, kids. Thank you all so much. You have no idea how much this means to me."

But I thought I had some sense of it.

I could still hear the echoes of her cries.

I hadn't forgotten.

"You all will be the hit of the crafts fair, I know it."

"Thanks, Aunt Lisa," I said.

"Anything you need. Anything at all. You just name it and I'll arrange it for you. Just say the word."

"We'll need something to build the barrier," I said.

"Maybe a cardboard box," Michelle said. "That's kind of like a lost thing."

"I can get you one," Aunt Lisa said.

Michelle turned to Violet and TJ. "We can decorate it with markers and beads."

"And socks," Violet added.

"Of course!"

"Those are our trademark items."

"We'll have to find a whole bunch of them that don't match."

Violet nodded to the pile she'd shoved to the floor. "Right."

The two of them were off and going, coming up with creative ways to decorate the barrier.

A barrier that would protect TJ from people.

I looked at Aunt Lisa, with tears in her eyes.

I looked at TJ, standing on the sidelines as Michelle and Violet brainstormed one idea after the next.

And I couldn't help it. I shuddered.

Something about this whole situation had me worried. Like we were on the verge of something truly terrible, something I couldn't avoid because I couldn't see it yet.

I couldn't deny what I was feeling. Not anymore.

I was afraid.

CHAPTER EIGHTEEN

I didn't want to let my fear stop me—especially since I didn't know what was causing it—so I threw myself into the project.

Both of my projects.

Thursday afternoon and all of Friday, we worked on the puppet show, coming up with everything we could possibly need. Most important, the story.

But both nights, after everyone had gone to bed, I slipped into the cabinet to read Aunt Lisa's binder. I was slowly working my way through her book *Psychological Trauma and Recovery*. It was a struggle. There were just so many words I didn't know. I tried to look up the terms on my phone, but each new word led to another round of links that I had to click, which pulled me further and further away from the book. Around and around I went. With nothing to show for it.

Except a growing sense of dread that I couldn't explain. And my newfound empathy, I guess.

Saturday and the Oak Lake crafts fair came almost as soon as Aunt Lisa's sticky buns were gone. Nicole texted me that morning:

Break a leg!

And a few minutes later, she texted again:

That's theatre talk for "good luck with your show!"

Frank Street was closed off with police barriers. And collapsible tables were lined up down the middle of the road, skirted with blue-and-white plastic tablecloths, decorated with red stars. They were back-to-back, with artists spreading out their work. Handmade jewelry. Glossy black-and-white photographs of cats and trees. Wooden block puzzles. Oil paintings of Paris and Vienna. Tie-dyed scarves. One booth had beautiful, old books, hollowed out and their pages glued together, hiding velvet-lined secret compartments. Open them up, expecting a story, and instead you'd get a surprise. Another booth housed a cartoonist, who sat customers on a stool and drew caricatures of them, exaggerating their teeth and foreheads and ears.

And it wasn't just art you could buy and hang on your wall.

Near the tracks, a little stage was set up. A local band, called Holly and the Millennials, was jamming out, playing covers of famous Dina and the Starlights songs.

You can sit under the bleachers
Or you can charge the field
But when I feel old doubts return
I grab my sword and my shield

In for a penny
In for a pound
You can't really lose
What was meant to be found

There was a cleared-out area in front of the stage, where kids were dancing and twirling around, making themselves dizzy with excitement.

Someone was blowing bubbles.

Someone even brought Hula-Hoops.

Beyond the stage, there were clusters of food stands. Fresh-squeezed lemonade. Cheddar- and caramel-coated popcorn. Kosher hot dogs with celery salt. A wide assortment of fancy cheesecakes. Tamales in corn husks. And, much to Aunt Lisa's delight, a stand selling individual slices of deep-dish pizza, oozing with gooey cheese and spicy sausage patties.

Most of the shops on the street were buzzing, their doors propped open to invite in the breeze and all the visitors who'd come from all over Chicago. They flew banners of green canvas, declaring their love for the Oak Lake neighborhood:

WELCOME TO OUR HOOD!
Take a break in Oak Lake!
ALL ARE WELCOME!

It made a lot of sense why Aunt Lisa loved this place so much.

Even the weather was cooperating today. It was summery, but with big, fat clouds. Warm enough that the water vendors were selling out of water bottles. But not so hot that the street was beginning to smell like sweat.

Mostly, it just smelled like sunblock.

Aunt Lisa set up the Lost Things Club's puppet stage at the very front of the fair, far enough away from the music that the audience would be able to hear us. I came up with the design for our stage myself. A cardboard box, built out of several cardboard boxes so it was big enough to hold three people. It was open on the sides, but the low front and the high back were closed off, creating a rectangular window for the puppets. When Michelle, Violet, and TJ crouched beneath the window, they could raise their arms and the puppets would appear, without any hint of the humans holding them up.

On the front of the box, we spelled out the name of our video series:

The Land of Lost Things

There were beads and buttons lining the letters. And then circling them was a rope of mismatched socks, tied together, heel to toe. We'd covered the cardboard with black construction paper, and dotted the background with tufts of lint, which looked like there were so many stars. Violet draped her patchwork quilt over the top of the whole thing.

It looked like a beautifully wrapped present.

Already, kids had started slowing down when they passed us, like they expected the gift to open itself.

Our first show wasn't until noon. Everything was set to go. Violet, TJ, and Michelle would operate the puppets in the box. My job would be to introduce the show and to fly in some of the scenery we'd whipped up. Nothing special.

A cardboard sun on a stick. A fluffy cloud made of lint, dangling from a string. A shooting star, lined with broken necklace chains.

My first almost-on-camera appearance.

Michelle was working on last-minute adjustments to the stage, regluing the lint and making sure the socks weren't coming loose and draping over our name. Violet's older sister, Katie, had agreed to lend a hand. Michelle greeted her warmly, although I noticed a tinge of sadness in Michelle's smile.

"What's wrong?" I asked her.

"Nothing," she said. "I just wish Jamal were here."

"He's not coming to the fair?"

"He doesn't like leaving his room, you know."

"Yeah, but for a few hours he could—"

"No." She shook her head. "Not at all."

I hadn't realized how serious she'd been. "Oh, I'm so—"

"It's all right," she said, turning away from me to continue working on the booth.

"Isolation." "Social anxiety." The words from Aunt Lisa's lists jumped to the forefront of my mind. I wondered if Michelle's mom had lists of her own.

Lists for Jamal.

I went to join Violet, who was busy checking out the crowd. Violet, of course, seemed to know everyone there, calling out and waving to classmates and neighbors, until suddenly, she grabbed my arm, her nails digging into my skin.

"What?" I said, looking at her.

"Over there," she whispered, nodding her head to the left.

I looked over. "What?" There was a frenzy of activity to the left—not to mention to the right and straight ahead—so I didn't have a clue what she was looking at.

"Do you see that woman?"

I saw several women. And Aunt Lisa.

Violet seemed to read my mind. "No, no," she said. "Not her. The woman your aunt is *talking* to."

She was wonderfully tall, with light brown skin and super dark, black hair. It was neatly arranged around her head in a crown of braids. She wore a bright red blazer on top, with a pair of skinny jeans.

"Who is she?" I asked.

"She's Julie Bruen."

"Julie Bruen?"

"Yeah." Violet rested her chin on top of my head, staring at Julie. "She's a reporter on WGN. There are pictures of her face all over the sides of buses."

"She looks cool," I said, squirming a little under Violet. Her chin, like the rest of her, was sharp and pointy.

"She's amazing," Violet replied. "My family watches her New Year's Eve TV special every year. It's the best.

She goes to Millennium Park and interviews all the guests. She once was onstage with Dina and the Starlights."

"Sounds like the kind of job you want to have someday."

"No kidding."

I smirked. "No wonder you like her."

"I don't like her," Violet said. "I *love* her."

"Well, that's a good thing."

"Why?"

"Because she's coming this way."

I heard Violet swallow a shriek. She immediately started smoothing down her hair. Both of us had allowed Michelle to braid keys into our hair so that we all matched. Violet started tugging at one now, taking quick, shallow breaths.

Aunt Lisa and Julie were, in fact, walking our way. Trailing behind them was a large man in a baseball hat, wearing a black shirt that had "WGN" across the front. Hoisted up on his shoulder was a gigantic camera. He dragged a cord along the ground. It slithered across the pavement, like a serpent.

"Here they are," Aunt Lisa said, as she got closer. "As you can see, Oak Lake is very proud of our own local celebrities."

"This is great," Julie said, looking at our puppet stage. She had the slightest hint of an accent, but I couldn't tell what it was. English, maybe. Or Australian or South African. I always got those three mixed up.

"Michelle, TJ," Aunt Lisa called, "come out here. There's someone I want you to meet."

Michelle came out from behind the stage. "Yeah?"

"Where's TJ?"

We all turned around to face the stage. "Hedgehog?" I said.

A small blond head poked out of the side of the box.

"There you are! Come over here, sweetie," Aunt Lisa said, beckoning.

TJ already had Staples on his hand. He crawled out of the box slowly, taking his time standing up straight, before shuffling over.

Aunt Lisa smiled at him, then turned to Julie. "These are the creative geniuses behind the videos. Violet Kowalski, Michelle Green, my niece Leah Abramowitz, and my little boy, Toby Isaac Cantor Jr. We call him 'TJ' for short."

Julie had amazing teeth. When she smiled, they were a little like looking at the sun. "Nice to meet you," she said. "Ladies, I love your hair." She offered her hand to each of us. Violet shook it a little too eagerly. It was far from the handshake she'd always practiced, and I had to cover my mouth to hide a smile. But TJ was standoffish, half ducking behind Michelle when he was offered the chance to shake Julie's hand, shrugging his shoulder up to his ear and turning to one side.

"He's shy," Michelle said, putting a hand on TJ's arm.

"I can see that," Julie said. She bent over, putting her hands on her knees, looking at him face-to-face. "Are you the boy behind Sir Staples the hedgehog?"

TJ nodded.

"You should know," Julie said, "he's my favorite character."

Violet gaped. "You watch our videos?" she asked.

"Watch them?" Julie laughed, straightening out. "I love them!"

I thought Violet might faint. Her cheeks turned bright pink and, for maybe the first time in her life, she was actually at a loss for words.

"Thank you," I said, covering for her.

"You're welcome."

"Julie was hoping that she might be able to ask you kids a couple of questions," Aunt Lisa said.

"And we'd like to record part of your show today," Julie added.

Michelle lit up. "You would?"

"We want to do a segment for the evening news on the crafts fair," she said. "And given how popular your videos are, we thought we'd focus on your appearance here." She paused. "If that's all right with you."

"Yes! Yes, it's all right!" Violet said. "Definitely all right. More than all right, really."

Julie laughed again. "I like that enthusiasm."

"Our show doesn't start until noon," Michelle said.

"That's fine. I'd actually love to talk to you before the show. Before you get rushed, I'm sure, by all your adoring fans. How would you kids feel about having an interview with me right now?"

"We're in!" Violet said.

"Fantastic."

I had no idea how complicated it was, sitting for an interview. But the cameraman—whose name was Jorge—first had us go to one side of the street, then the other. Trying to line up a shot. Trying to figure out a way to get the fair and the stage in the background.

"Pay close attention," he said to me, as he set his camera on a tripod. "You're the director for the Land of Lost Things, aren't you?"

The director.

I'd never thought about myself by that word before, but I kind of liked it. It felt very sophisticated. Very important, somehow.

Special.

And it felt *right*.

"Yeah," I said. "Yes, I am. I'm the director. It's what I do."

Jorge winked at me. "Well, come over here. Take a look in the lens. This is how you line up an exterior shot."

I stood up on my tiptoes and watched the way he adjusted the camera on the tripod, while Julie stood in different places, the light on her face changing, depending on the way it filtered through the trees.

When Jorge was finally happy with the angle of the camera, he had all of us stand in a line beside Julie. Julie was holding a handheld microphone, with the big WGN logo on it, but Jorge clipped battery-operated microphones to the front of our shirts. "It can be hard to hear with all this background noise," he told me. "These should pick up everything you say that the handheld misses. And I'll tell you the ultimate secret to this kind of shoot."

"What?" I asked.

He reached into his pocket and pulled out three double-A batteries. "Always have extras. Just in case."

A second person in a WGN shirt, a woman with long green hair, came over to Julie, applying a bit of powder to her nose and forehead. Violet watched the whole thing with such an intense longing that the woman offered to give her a touch-up, too. She used a soft pad and quickly brushed some makeup on Violet's face.

"All right," Julie said, what felt like hours later, "I think we're more or less set up. We're not going to film this live,

253

so don't worry. If you mess up, just say you want to start again and you can start again. We'll edit the whole thing later."

Aunt Lisa, standing behind Jorge, gave us two thumbs-up.

"Just act natural," Julie continued. "Don't worry about the camera. Just look at me. And remember, have fun. You aren't getting graded or anything. There are no right or wrong answers."

Violet was drinking it in.

"Okay," Jorge said. "We'll start rolling in five, four, three…" He didn't say "two" or "one." He just held up his hand and pointed to Julie.

Julie transformed in an instant. Her posture was straighter, her shoulders level and formal. She smiled a big toothy smile, staring into the lens of the camera she'd told us to ignore. "Julie Bruen here. I'm visiting one of the many fantastic, local summer events to check out this year. I'm at the Oak Lake crafts fair with some very promising young Chicagoans. Joining me is the creative team behind the Land of Lost Things, the popular video series making the rounds on YouTube. With their quirky characters and their world made entirely out of the lost-and-found box, these stories are capturing the hearts of—"

"Not stories."

It was TJ. He looked up at Julie with a fierce glare.

Again, I remembered that term I'd read in Aunt Lisa's binder again. "Trigger words." Julie had just used one.

Julie's camera persona faded and she looked down at him, puzzled, but not upset. "What?"

"They're not stories. Don't call them stories."

Aunt Lisa took a step up, rising on her toes over Jorge's shoulder. "I think he prefers it when you call them 'videos,'" she said, with that forced lightness in her voice.

"Oh." Julie nodded. "Well, all right." She looked at Jorge. "Where do you want to pick up?"

"Go from 'Joining me,'" Jorge said.

She nodded. And composed herself again. Like a light, she was "on." "Joining me is the creative team behind the Land of Lost Things, the popular video series making the rounds on YouTube. With their quirky characters and their world made entirely out of the lost-and-found box, these *videos* are capturing the hearts of thousands." Julie turned to us. "Why don't you introduce yourselves?"

"I'm Violet Kowalski," Violet said. "I'm twelve years old, and I'm going to be in seventh grade, and when I get older, I want to be—"

"And who do you play, Violet?"

"I play Queen Queenie the Fifth," she said. I noticed that she was holding herself up straighter. Copying Julie's posture.

But Julie shifted, turning to Michelle. "And you are?"

"Michelle Green," she said. "I'm Francis the flamingo."

Julie turned to me. "And?"

"Leah Abramowitz," I said. "I'm...the director."

Jorge gave me a thumbs-up with his free hand.

"And certainly the youngest director I've ever seen," Julie said. She smiled over at TJ. "And you are?"

TJ just stared at her.

Quickly, Michelle leaned over. "This is TJ Cantor. He plays Sir Staples the Brave."

"Hello, TJ," Julie said. She straightened up again. "The Land of Lost Things has put a spotlight on the Oak Lake neighborhood. Viewers are transported to an imaginary land called the Land of—"

"No," TJ cut in.

Julie looked at him again. "No?"

"It's not imaginary."

"TJ!" Aunt Lisa said.

He ignored her, glaring at Julie in a way I'd never seen before. The way he'd yelled at his parents in their bedroom was nothing compared to this. Maybe because she was a stranger. Or maybe because something was changing in TJ.

"It's not imaginary," he said. "Redo it. Take it back. Pick another word."

I had to do something.

But what?

Julie looked over at Aunt Lisa. And then at TJ. "All right," she said. "Is there another word you'd like? How about 'fictional'?"

"No," he said.

"'Make-believe'?"

"No."

"'Fantastic'?"

"Stop it!"

TJ shouted. Actually shouted. The kind of shouting that happened with his whole body. Mouth wide, feet planted, face red. A couple of fairgoers passing by paused, looking over. But TJ didn't care.

"Stop using words like that," he continued, his voice only getting louder. "Stop using words that make it sound like it isn't true!"

"Hedgehog—" I started.

He ignored me. "The Land of Lost Things is real. You can't say that it's not real. It is real! It is!"

"Toby Isaac Cantor Jr.," Aunt Lisa said, stepping around the camera. "You know better than to—"

"I do know better!" TJ said. "I know better than all of you! I know it's real!"

Julie seemed at a loss. She signaled for Jorge to stop filming. He put his hand in front of the lens.

"It exists!" Tears were streaming down TJ's face all of

a sudden, glistening in the sunlight. "The Land of Lost Things is real!"

Aunt Lisa looked mortified. "You know that it's not—"

"I know!" TJ shouted. "I know and it's never going to be not real! It's always going to be real! Always!"

With that, he grabbed the microphone pinned to his shirt and ripped it off, throwing it down on the sidewalk. He turned and ran, darting between a man walking his dog and a couple admiring a booth of photographs.

"TJ!" Aunt Lisa screamed.

But already, he'd disappeared into the crowd. He was so little, it was all too easy to lose him.

I looked at Violet and Michelle.

An understanding passed between us.

"We'll get him, Aunt Lisa," I said, taking off my mic and setting it down gently.

The three of us took off.

Somehow, I knew this was what I'd been dreading.

CHAPTER NINETEEN

It was hard to keep running through the fair. There were just so many people, going in a thousand different directions all at once. Violet, Michelle, and I kept having to dodge around them, jangling like wind chimes caught in a storm. We got separated and came back together. We had a few near collisions, as people walking their bikes across the road blocked our way. As hard as I tried to hold on to Violet and Michelle, we kept getting ripped apart.

And we were operating on pure instinct.

None of us could see TJ.

It was useless to call out his name. There's no way he would have heard us.

And even if he had...

Well. I knew he wasn't going to answer.

But I kept running, pumping my arms to either side, determined not to lose him. If I'd ever put this much effort into running in gym, I would have passed the Presidential Youth Fitness Program for sure.

But that didn't matter.

This did.

We tore past the stage, where Holly and the Millennials were singing, crashing through a group of kids dancing in our way.

> *In for a penny*
> *In for a pound*
> *You can't really lose*
> *What was meant to be found*

"Sorry, Samantha!" Violet called over her shoulder, at an annoyed redhead with a Hula-Hoop flipped over her shoulders.

We plunged into the cool shade of the train tracks, colliding into a group of college students in matching purple-and-white shirts who'd just walked down the stairs from the train platform.

And that's when someone said, "Hey, Cousin!"

It was Morgan.

He was arranging a couple of jelly-filled doughnuts in

a pink box for a woman in a big floppy hat, looking surprisingly at ease. He gave me one of his crooked smiles, waving me over with two fingers.

I shook my head. "I'm sorry, Morgan. We can't talk right now."

"We're in a hurry!" Violet said.

"Looking for little man?" Morgan asked.

"Yeah," Michelle said.

Morgan nodded. "I saw him go by."

"Do you know where he went?" Violet asked.

"Sure do," Morgan said. "And you do, too."

We looked at one another. And reached the same conclusion at the exact same moment, I think. "The laundromat," I said.

And we were off and running again.

Squeaky Green wasn't part of the fair. No, the fair ended right by the tracks. But there were a ton of people hanging out on the sidewalk outside, anyway. People who hadn't been able to find a place to sit and eat in the fair itself. People coming. People going. And, of course, people just having their regular days, who didn't care about the fair at all.

We cut through them, grabbing one another by the hands, as we dove into the front door of the laundromat.

Sir Staples the Brave was abandoned on the floor in front of us, his quills pointing in a hundred different directions.

The silver brave heart had fallen off him, trampled and crinkled, it seemed, by tiny, running feet on a tiny, running boy.

A few of the laundromat regulars were there. But none of them were chatting or separating or folding. They stood along the sides of the walls, staring at the back wall of dryers. Dryer number five was open wide, its mouth gaping and yawning.

And TJ was on the floor in front of it.

Well, sort of on the floor.

We could see his legs, kicking and jerking, but the rest of him was inside the dryer.

And he was screaming.

The sound of his cries echoed through the room, off the cold, metal surfaces of the machines.

I let go of Violet and Michelle, running over to where he was.

There were eyes on us. As hard as they fought not to stare, they couldn't help it. They didn't understand why a kid would throw himself into a dryer.

But I did.

I knew where he was trying to go.

I tried to block them all out.

When I got to the dryers, I crouched down. TJ was screaming and screaming, and didn't even know I was there until I reached around his waist, pulling him gently out of the dryer. He tried to jerk away from me, but I was stronger. I held him hard against my chest.

He just kept screaming.

His forehead was pink, a lump rising where he'd slammed his head. His face was slippery with sweat and tears, twisted into an unnatural shape, like a jack-o'-lantern at Halloween. He continued to shriek, even as I hugged him tight, feeling his heart beat against my skin. Violet and Michelle dropped down to the floor on either side of us, putting their hands on his shoulders. It didn't help.

I'm not sure he felt it.

"Hedgehog," I whispered, pressing my lips to his ear, giving him the lightest of kisses. "Hedgehog..."

"No!" he screamed. He didn't look at me or grab my arms or try to wipe my germs away. "No! No!"

"Hey," Michelle said. "TJ..."

"It's all right, TJ," Violet told him.

"It's not all right!" He shook his head fiercely, his curls plastered to his skin with sweat. "It's not all right!"

With that, he let out another yowl.

"What is it, buddy?" Michelle asked, desperately curling her fingers into his shoulder.

"You can tell us," Violet said.

"The portal won't let me in!" He thrashed, although I'm not sure what he was hoping to do, exactly. He couldn't break away. And he couldn't push me back. I guess he was too upset to hold still. Like his body would explode if he didn't keep moving around. "I can't get into the Land of Lost Things!"

I looked into the gaping maw of the dryer and saw a light, oily smear against the back of the metal wall, shining in rainbow colors. Where TJ must have hit his forehead, diving headfirst into where he thought the portal was.

My fingers brushed against his forehead. It throbbed under my fingers.

"I have to go there!" he shouted. "I have to get to the Land of Lost Things!"

"TJ," Michelle said, "there's no reason to get upset."

"Yeah," Violet said. "It was only a game."

But all three of us knew it was more than a game. At least for TJ. We'd all known for some time.

"No!" He practically snarled at her, turning so fast that I actually thought he was going to bite her hand. But Violet pulled away, falling back onto her palms, and TJ buried his face in my shoulder. "It's not just a game! It's not!"

"But—"

"No, Violet," I said. "Don't."

She shut her mouth.

We were standing on the brink of the part of the story I'd been missing. The part we'd all been missing. For us, the Land of Lost Things was just fun. But it meant something else to TJ. Something real. Something important.

Something worth leaving the world behind for.

It was time to know what that was.

TJ started screaming again. He threw his head back and wailed.

Listen to kids. All the lists said that. *Listen.*

I'd been listening.

I just hadn't bothered to ask the right questions.

"Hedgehog," I whispered, squeezing him tight. "Tell me why. Tell me why it's so important to you. Why do you have to go to the Land of Lost Things?"

"Because I lost something, and I have to get it back!"

With that, he wrenched himself loose. I guess I was too confused to hang on. Like a wild animal, he crawled on his hands and knees back to the dryer, shoving himself into it. He didn't hit his head this time. But we could hear him pounding his fists against the back of the dryer.

"Let me in! Let me in!"

"TJ!" Michelle shouted.

Violet and I both grabbed him around the middle and pulled him out.

He clutched the lip of the dryer, clinging on until his

fingers turned white, trying to pull himself back. It took Michelle's help for the three of us to get him out, breaking a few of his nails as he clutched at the dryer.

"Let me go!" he said. "I have to go there! I have to!"

"You can't, TJ," Violet said.

"I can!"

"No, Hedgehog," I said. I smoothed down his hair, rocking him back and forth against my arm. "No..."

TJ looked up to Michelle. Michelle, who he always turned to first. Michelle, who had created a whole world for him. Michelle, who told the story with such passion that it had to be true. His rainy-day eyes stared into hers. Between the tears, he silently begged her. Please.

Please.

Michelle bit her lips together. And just barely shook her head.

No.

No, he couldn't go.

No, it wasn't real.

TJ tossed his head back and howled.

Michelle crawled over and threw her arms around the both of us. And Violet was there in the next second. We huddled in a tight cluster on the floor.

And we let TJ scream.

It was what he wanted.

Or maybe what he needed.

I wasn't sure.

But it went on and on and on.

One of the regular customers of the laundromat, a handsome guy with longish hair, tried to move closer. "Do you need—"

"It's fine," Violet said, with the same ferocity she used to scare drivers away from her parking spot.

Holding up his hands, the regular quickly backed away. "Should I get Ms. Green?" he asked.

"No," Michelle said.

I guess she figured having her mom around would only make things more complicated than they already were.

Adults couldn't help TJ.

Only we could.

There were others still watching, scared and uncertain. Violet glared around the room, daring any of them to approach.

Not a single one did.

TJ kept screaming. Until he suddenly couldn't scream anymore. He grabbed his throat with both hands and started gagging. Coughing. Choking.

"TJ!" I shouted. "No, TJ. No!"

"Breathe!" Michelle said.

"In and out." Violet took a deep breath and let it out. She ran her hand up and down the front of her chest, doing it again and again.

He watched her, his face turning nearly purple until he took a deep breath. And then another. And another. He was breathing again, but then he started to cry. He sobbed. And with his tears, I felt some of my own building up. But it didn't last long. He grew quiet and still. And in a matter of minutes or hours, he'd cried himself dry.

The last of his tears landed on the Formica floor of the laundromat.

And TJ fell asleep in our arms.

CHAPTER TWENTY

He slept.

But he didn't really rest.

His eyelashes fluttered against his cheeks. His eyes shifted from one side to another. And he kept making... noises.

We carried him into the back room. The unofficial clubhouse for the Lost Things Club. I sent off a text to Aunt Lisa, telling her that TJ was fine and we were going to calm him down. She wanted to know where we were right away, but I didn't answer. It was selfish of me. Wrong. I knew that. But all the same, there was an instinct whispering in my ears, telling me that Aunt Lisa wasn't going to help the situation.

Not yet, anyway.

He didn't need an adult hovering over him.

He needed the Lost Things Club.

I insisted on keeping TJ with me, on my lap. Michelle and Violet came and went. Michelle left to tell her mom what had happened, before one of the customers could. She returned with sandwiches and water. Violet fetched her sun-warmed blanket from the puppet stage to wrap up TJ. We didn't really talk. But we were there for one another. And there for TJ.

After a while, he started to fuss even more.

At first, it was just fitful dreaming sounds. He moaned softly. Let out little sobs. Little grunts.

Trouble sleeping. That was a symptom of trauma.

But slowly he woke up, his eyelashes sticking together a little bit with sweat and tears and eye goop.

"Hi, Hedgehog," I said, running my hand through his curls.

"Where are we?" he asked drowsily, blinking.

"The clubhouse," Michelle said.

"You were sleeping for a while," Violet added.

"Sleeping?" We watched as the memories returned to him. The howling. The bump on his head. The back of the dryer, solid and unforgiving under his fists. His little face crumpled up, but he had no tears left to cry.

"It's okay," I said, cupping his cheek in my hand. It was hot and clammy. "It's going to be okay."

"No," he said. "It's not going to be okay."

"Why not?"

"Because…because…" He made a few dry, hacking noises. "Because if the Land of Lost Things isn't real, then…"

"Sh, sh, sh." I kissed his forehead. "Easy does it."

"If the Land of Lost Things isn't real—"

"Then what?" Violet asked. "It doesn't matter."

But it did matter. I could feel his urgency, his *need*. It mattered to him very, very much.

He looked up at me. "Then I can't go there. I can't go there and rescue Jeremiah."

What?

I looked up at the other two. Michelle's forehead was scrunched up. But Violet's eyes slowly started to widen.

"Jeremiah," she said.

"Who?" I asked.

"TJ," Violet said, scooting closer on her hands and knees. "Do you mean Jeremiah Jamison?"

He nodded.

"Who is that?" I looked back and forth between the two of them.

Michelle clapped a hand over her mouth.

"Jeremiah Jamison," Violet said, "was the boy we lost at Chancelor. During the..."

During the shooting.

We'd known all along that it was something about the shooting that was troubling TJ.

Why hadn't I thought to ask what actually happened?

Violet had told me a boy had died.

But that boy hadn't been TJ.

So I'd forgotten all about it. All about him. He was nothing to me. Just a sad fact to file away.

But TJ hadn't forgotten.

I looked down at TJ. "What does the Land of Lost Things have to do with Jeremiah Jamison?"

"He's there," TJ said. "Like Morgan used to be. He's lost. And I have to go find him. I have to bring him back."

Aunt Lisa's binder had said something about that. It had warned not to use words like "lost."

Seemed like someone had used it anyway: We *lost* Jeremiah. That's what someone had told TJ.

Maybe even a lot of someones.

And TJ didn't understand. "Lost" didn't mean *lost*. It meant that Jeremiah wasn't coming back. It meant there was nothing TJ could do.

But why had TJ put that responsibility on himself? He said that *he* had lost Jeremiah.

"Why?" I asked. "Why do you think you have to bring him back?"

"Because it's my *fault*."

I looked to Violet again, but she had nothing for me. She shook her head.

Michelle squeezed her eyes shut.

I looked back at TJ. "TJ, why would you say that?"

He snuffled a little, rubbing his eyes with the back of his hand. "We got in a fight," he said. "He was wearing new gym shoes, and I told him they were ugly, so he said I was just jealous. I wasn't jealous, though. They really *were* ugly. And I kept saying that, but he wouldn't listen to me, so I pushed him."

"You pushed him?"

He nodded. "And Mr. Hiler saw it, so he called us to the front of the room. And I said it was all Jeremiah's fault, but he said it was all my fault. And Mr. Hiler said that since I was the one who pushed him, I had to go to the principal's office."

Just like Violet said.

TJ was in the principal's office at the time of the shooting.

"And..." TJ's eyes were getting watery again. Apparently, he still had a few tears left, after all.

"And?" I asked him.

"And Mr. Hiler made Jeremiah sit in the front of the class. By the door."

The pieces fell into place, locking with a sickening sound.

It must have been the place Jeremiah was sitting when the shooting happened. When he got killed.

While TJ was far away, in the safe nest of the principal's office.

"Oh, TJ," I whispered. I took his face in my hands again, pulling it close, so I could rest my forehead against his.

"It's all my fault," TJ said. "He's lost because of me. I was mean, and now he's lost and that isn't fair. But then Michelle told me about the Land of Lost Things. Lost things can be found again. I know it. Jeremiah can come h-home."

"This isn't the same kind of lost."

"TJ," Michelle said, speaking through the hand over her mouth. "TJ, I am so, so sorry." She turned to me, her eyes big and frightened. "I never meant for him to—"

"I know," I cut her off.

Michelle didn't have a cruel bone in her body. It wasn't her fault.

"He was sad," she said. "I thought the stories were cheering him up again. I used to tell stories about the Land of Lost Things to my little brother all the time. I missed telling them. I missed being a big sister. I was just trying to help. I was lonely. That's all it was."

"You have nothing to apologize for," I told her.

"I think I do. I thought I was making him better, but I was just—"

"You were doing what you thought was right," Violet said. "What you thought would help."

Just like me.

I'd wanted to help, too.

We all had good intentions. There wasn't a bad guy here.

"I didn't see what was right in front of me," Michelle said.

"None of us did."

TJ turned his face to them. "What are you saying? What do you mean?"

"Hedgehog," I said. "I know this is going to be hard for you to believe, but you have to listen to me very carefully."

"What?"

I took a deep breath. "What happened to Jeremiah was terrible but it wasn't your fault."

"It was!"

"No!" I gave him a squeeze. "It wasn't your fault. Okay? You didn't bring a gun into the school. You didn't pull a trigger. You didn't take anyone's *life*."

There. I'd said it.

Jeremiah was dead.

TJ couldn't bring him back home.

It was the truth, and I felt *awful*.

We could see TJ slowly beginning to understand. He was a smart kid. He knew what dead meant. "But then..."

"What?"

"But then I'm even worse!" TJ's lower lip trembled. "If it hadn't been for me, he wouldn't have been sitting in front."

"And someone else would have been," I said. Which was another terrible thing to say to a little kid. But that didn't make it any less true. "What happened to Jeremiah, what could have happened to any other kid, that's on the person who did this. That's on the person who chose to take his anger out with a gun, instead of with stories."

"But I want to fix it."

"There isn't anyone on this planet who doesn't want to fix it, TJ," I said. "But you can't undo the past. You can only live in the present."

"And try to fix the future," Violet added.

"How am I supposed to do that?"

"You tell the story." It was Michelle who said it. In her soft, soothing voice.

TJ shuddered. "No more stories," he said.

"Yes, more stories," she replied. "That's how people listen to things. That's how people learn to feel. It's the language of the human race. Look at how you got people to pay attention to you, just with a talking hedgehog. Everyone wants to hear stories."

"This isn't a happy story," TJ said. "It's not good."

"Stories don't have to be happy to be good," she said. "You tell your story. People are going to listen. And maybe, just maybe, they'll change something because of it. Or change themselves."

"I don't know."

"You don't have to know now, TJ," I said. "It's okay not to know."

He gave me a wary look. "But?"

I smiled. At least, I think I did. I couldn't feel it. "You know me so well." I sighed. "*But.* I think, if nothing else, you should probably tell your story to two particular people."

"Mommy and Daddy?" he asked.

"Yeah."

His eyes drooped. "Oh."

"TJ, they're worried about you. They need to know what's going on in here." I tapped the side of his head with my fingertips. "And they want to help you feel better in here." I touched his chest. "But they can't do that if they don't know the whole story."

"She's right," Violet said.

Michelle nodded. "Yeah. Remember what we said before? That's how a story gains power. From being told."

That felt long ago.

Our adventure had started out so innocently.

But innocence had also been lost to the Land of Lost Things.

Another tear slid down the side of TJ's face.

I was a little surprised it was only one tear.

After that, there were no more.

He rubbed his eyes with the backs of his hands, sitting up straight on my lap. Violet started to smooth down his hair. And Michelle reached out her hand, offering him something.

Sir Staples the Brave.

Michelle had brushed him off and filled up his round, little body with lint. Not a puppet anymore. Just a stuffed friend.

The silver heart gleamed on his chest.

TJ took him from her and held him against his own heart.

CHAPTER TWENTY-ONE

I visited Oak Lake once more, near the end of the summer. My mom had some paperwork she wanted to go over with Uncle Toby, and I asked if I could tag along to see TJ. The second she said yes, I sent a couple of texts to Violet and Michelle. Both of them immediately agreed to meet up one last time.

The Lost Things Club couldn't really make any new videos when I was all the way in Deerwood Park and the rest of them were in the city. Well, we *could*. But they wouldn't be the same. Still, the three of us had kept in touch. And in our time apart, somehow, we managed to come up with an idea for our best project yet, better than any of our other videos. All we needed was the opportunity to see one another.

An opportunity I finally managed to wrangle, about a week before school was going to start again.

My mom and I arrived in the early morning and were pleasantly surprised to find a nice, wide parking space waiting for us, right in front of Uncle Toby and Aunt Lisa's apartment building.

As if someone had saved it for us.

Out of politeness, we let Aunt Lisa buzz us up. She was waiting at the top of the stairs when we got there. "Good morning, Hannah. Good morning, Leah."

"Hello, Lisa," my mom said.

"Leah! Leah!" TJ came bowling into the living room before I'd even had the chance to walk into the apartment. He threw himself into my arms, giving me such a powerful hug that I thought I might fall over.

"Easy does it, TJ," Aunt Lisa said. "You don't want to throw her down the stairs."

"Sorry," TJ said, pulling back just enough so I could breathe.

I ruffled his hair. "Hi, Hedgehog."

"Is that my baby sister and my favorite Illinois niece?" Uncle Toby came bounding into the room, carrying something bulky under his arm.

"Hi, Toby," my mom said.

"Hi, Uncle Toby," I echoed.

He gave each of us a kiss. "Look what I have, favorite

Illinois niece," he said. From under his arm, he produced the drone. It was finally finished, all of the pieces in place.

"It looks great, Uncle Toby."

He looked so proud of himself, I didn't have the heart to tell him that a couple of the props looked like they were upside down. He handed the drone to TJ. "Come back to my study, Hannah. Let's take a look at the mess we have on our hands." He gave me a little wink. "And you, why don't you take your little cousin for a walk?"

"Take him for a walk?" Aunt Lisa said, shaking her head. "He's not a puppy, Toby!"

"No, *bubbeleh*," Uncle Toby said. "You heard what Leah said. He's a hedgehog."

She groaned, but seemed to be smiling.

Really smiling. In a way I hadn't seen all summer.

As the grown-ups disappeared into the study, TJ stood up on his tiptoes and whispered into my ear, "The drone won't fly. I really, really don't think Daddy was ever in the CIA, Leah."

I covered my mouth to stop myself from giggling.

The late August trees were still full and thick, although a few of the leaves had started to lose that perfect, vibrant shade of green. They'd be yellow and orange and red in a few weeks.

The summer was over.

"Ms. Weinstein makes me write in my journal every night, before I go to bed," TJ was telling me. It didn't sound like his time with her was a whole lot of fun, but he wasn't running away anymore. And he wasn't quite so quiet. I knew those were both good things. "She says I'm the best writer she's ever had."

"Probably because of all that practice your mommy makes you do," I told him, swinging our arms, our fingers interlaced as we crossed the street. "You're lucky you have a teacher for a mommy."

TJ rolled his eyes. *"Lucky."*

I smiled slightly. "What do you write about?"

"Ms. Weinstein tells me to write about how I feel about different things," he said. "Like, what makes me happy and what makes me sad each day. She calls it the 'story of the day.' Although it's not always a very interesting story."

"And what makes you happy?"

"Mommy's sticky buns."

I laughed. "And?"

"My library books."

"Makes sense. And sad? What makes you sad?"

He shrugged. "Thinking about Jeremiah."

"Yeah." I nodded. "It's good that you understand that," I said.

"That's what Ms. Weinstein says."

"Well, if she says it and I say it, then it must be right."

He laughed.

We crossed under the train tracks. I was surprised when I didn't see Morgan there, sitting on his milk crate, waiting for customers. Instead, there was a young woman in his apron and visor, absently scrolling through her phone as she leaned against the wall, behind the register. She didn't notice us.

"Hey, Hedgehog. Where'd Morgan go?" I asked, nodding toward the shop.

"I don't know," TJ said. "He stopped being around a little while after you left."

"Excuse me?" I said to the woman on her phone.

She glanced up at us from beneath heavy eyelashes. "Yeah?"

"Where's Morgan?"

"Who?"

I gestured to the shop. "The guy who usually works here."

The woman shrugged. "I don't know. On vacation. Something about visiting family, somewhere. Or something."

She obviously didn't care.

I put my hand on TJ's shoulder. As we continued to walk, I leaned in close so only he could hear. "Maybe he found his flying bathtub and flew away," I said.

TJ wrinkled his nose at me. "Flying bathtubs aren't real," he pointed out.

"I know," I said. "But maybe he found a real way home."

We might never know for sure. But it was a pleasant thought.

The rest of the walk to Squeaky Green was quiet, both of us probably imagining the very best possible ending for Morgan's story. The little bell over the door rang as we walked in. But neither of us heard it ring again as the door closed behind us, because we were suddenly attacked from all sides.

"TJ!"

"And Leah!"

"Hi, you guys!"

"What took you so long?"

Violet and Michelle swooped in on us in a flurry of hugs, and the four of us quickly became a tangled knot of limbs. When we finally managed to break free, I smiled at the two of them. Violet, if it was even possible, seemed to have grown an extra inch in the weeks apart. And Michelle had taken the keys out of her hair, replacing them with buttons from her collection. Not quite as shiny, but definitely a lot less noisy.

I knew they'd been spending a lot of time together since I left for Deerwood Park. Michelle was helping Violet write down the story of our summer together. And

Violet was helping Michelle to pull together all the materials she would need for her high school applications next year. It was strange to think of Violet—her eyes forever on the future—taking some time to reflect on the past. And Michelle, always dreamy about the past, putting some thought into her future. They were good for each other, that way.

We'd all brought something out of one another.

"Come on, come on!" Violet said. "We don't have a minute to lose!" She grabbed TJ by the hand and tugged him in the direction of the wall of dryers.

"What are you talking about?" TJ asked, stumbling along after her.

"Our video," Michelle said, trotting behind them.

"What video?"

"The final one," Violet said.

"At least for now," Michelle added.

"We need a season finale," I said, hopping up on one of the washing machines, my phone out and ready.

TJ looked over his shoulder, his eyes scrunching in suspicion. "Why are we doing a video?"

I gave him a tiny smile. "It's what we do."

"I left Staples at home."

"That's all right," Violet said. "You won't need him for this."

"How do you know?" he asked.

"Because *someone*"—she gave me a tiny smirk—"finally realized that everything would go much better if we had an actual script. Instead of just making it up in the moment."

"There's a script?"

Michelle reached into the pocket of her oversized magenta overalls and pulled out a folded sheet of paper. "Here it is."

"And everyone has seen it except for me?"

"I rehearsed my lines with Jamal last night," Michelle said. "He says it's the best episode yet."

I liked knowing that. Knowing that Jamal had been watching this whole time.

"We've been memorizing our lines all week," Violet told TJ.

TJ pouted. "But how am I supposed to memorize mine?" he asked.

"Don't worry," Violet told him. "You only have one written line. But it's the most important one. So we should probably practice before we start."

Michelle and Violet sat down on either side of dryer number five, its door hanging open. They left a space between them, and Violet patted it eagerly, but TJ stood where he was, his hands on his hips, looking so much like Aunt Lisa that I nearly started giggling. "But where's Queenie? And Francis?"

"No Queenie," Michelle said. "No Francis." She held out the folded script to him. "Take a look, buddy."

He took the paper from her and unfolded it. He read only a couple lines before he whirled around to face me. "This says no puppets. This says our real faces."

"Yeah," I said.

"But we're not supposed to show our real faces."

"It's all right, TJ," I said. "I talked to your mommy and daddy, and they said it was all right to show real faces for this. Remember? Your mommy was going to let us show real faces for the interview for WGN."

Violet sighed wistfully.

Michelle nudged her.

TJ opened his mouth. Then closed it. "Oh."

"Now, go sit with Michelle and Violet," I told him. "I have to get you all in the shot."

Studying the script, TJ walked over and plopped down between them.

I tried to remember some of the fancy tricks that Jorge, the WGN cameraman, showed me for setting up a shot. But none of them really made a lot of sense when we were inside and the light wasn't really changing all that much. I would definitely remember his tricks when I got back to school, though. I was kind of thinking about joining our film and theatre club. I wasn't exactly ready to give up being a director just yet. I liked it. And maybe I was even good at it.

If nothing else, it had given me a taste of being special.

Maybe not to the world. But special to the people who mattered to me.

Which seemed like a good start.

"What's this part, here at the end?" TJ asked, pointing down at the bottom of the script. "Where it says 'TJ tells his story'?"

Violet's idea. Well, mine, but only because of something she'd said to me: *Every person has some kind of story.*

"Right, so," Michelle said. "That's kind of up to you. We wanted to give you the chance to tell your story. About the day of the shooting."

"But only if you *want* to," Violet added.

"Oh."

The three of us watched him, all thinking the same thing, wondering how he would feel about it. I was the one brave enough to ask. "Do you want to, Hedgehog?"

TJ bit down on his lower lip. And then he nodded. Only slightly. But he nodded. "Yeah, I think so."

"No pressure," Violet said.

"Let's practice the first part, okay?"

"Sounds good," Michelle said.

"Get that right before I..." He trailed off.

"Tell your story? Remember, you don't have to."

"I'm ready," he said.

I wiggled back on the washer just slightly, steadied the phone, and nodded to them to begin.

"Hello, everyone!" Michelle said, waving her hand at the camera. "This is the Lost Things Club."

"School's about to start up again, which means that this is the end of the first season of the Land of Lost Things," Violet said. "But don't think that you won't be hearing from us again. Season two is just a summer away."

"Before we wrap up, we wanted to take a second to thank you all for following us," Michelle continued. "You watched. You commented. You shared. And the Land of Lost Things would be nothing without all of you."

They both turned to look at TJ. Suddenly shy again, I worried that TJ wouldn't speak. But after a second or two of hesitation, he swallowed hard and looked up at the camera. "We want to dedicate our first season to the memory of Jeremiah Jamison," he said. His voice was soft at first, but it started to grow. He looked down at the script, and then up again. "Jeremiah was a special person in our lives, and he brought us all together. He was killed in the shooting at Chancelor Elementary School. We'll miss him every day. But we hope that his memory will stay alive forever."

My arms came down, resting the camera in my lap. It

was so important to have real faces on-screen for this. The three of them were survivors of something terrible. People needed to see them. Not just to remember. Not just in the hope that something so awful would never happen to kids like them again. But also to understand that there was a life to live after surviving. And the three of them were figuring out how to do just that.

We sat in silence. And I figured they were all thinking the same thing. Or something like it, anyway.

My empathy told me that.

"What do you think, Leah?" Michelle asked. "Good rehearsal?"

"I think it's perfect," I said.

"Then we should roll," Violet said.

"Hang on a second," TJ said. He got to his feet and turned to face the dryer. After a moment of hesitation, he closed the door with a snap. "That's better," he said, sitting down again. "Now, you have to give us a 'Lights! Camera! Action!' this time, okay?"

"Okay," I said with a smile.

"So we know that it's for real."

"I will," I said.

"Good."

True to my word, I raised the camera again and gave them the "Lights! Camera! Action!"

And I started to record the end of our story.

I guess I'd predicted my future after all, staring at that grid of letters in the back seat of my mom's car: "Journey." "Surprises." "Story." Those were my three words. And each of them had somehow managed to come true. I'd gone on a journey full of surprises and lived to tell the story.

Or maybe we'd written that story ourselves.

ACKNOWLEDGMENTS

First I need to thank my mother. If you've read *Captain Superlative*, you already know why.

Writing a book might look, on the surface, like a solo endeavor, but there are so many people involved, and each of them brings something critical, vital, and exciting to every draft. A big thank-you to my agent, Brianne Johnson, and the team at Writers House, for continuing to believe in me and the stories I have to tell. This book would never have happened without Tracey Keevan and her early enthusiasm and editorial thoughts, and Samantha Gentry at Little, Brown Books for Young Readers, who passionately drove the story home. Thank you to Erica Ferguson for the incredible and thorough copyedit, which included repeating all my gnarly Google and Wikipedia searches! Additional thanks to copy chief Jen Graham and proofreader Lori Lewis for a thorough polish of the text. James Gulliver Hancock, your cover amazes me every time I look at it.

This novel was guided along by my support network of friends. Stephanie Kaplan and Meg Bullock, without you calming me down every time I freaked out about what my second novel was going to be, I would never have found the peace of mind to actually sit down and write it! Thank you to Carly Ho and her whole NaNoWriMo Discord group for being an occasional sounding board. Nicole Keating, you continue to be my muse.

I want to thank all my colleagues at the University of Chicago Consortium on School Research. Their continued dedication to improving educational outcomes for students in Chicago and beyond is inspiring. And their research guided me along every single draft. A special thanks to Camille A. Farrington, Joseph Maurer, Meredith R., Aska McBride, Jenny Nagaoka, Steve Shewfelt, Elizabeth M. Weiss, and Lindsay Wright for letting me take part in the arts education project. *Arts Education and Social-Emotional Learning Outcomes Among K–12 Students* became an unexpected backbone of this story.

I want to thank LeVar Burton. I've never actually met him and I probably never will, but I thought it would be cool to include someone as awesome and awe-inspiring, who has done more for childhood literacy than any Starfleet officer I can think of. And I'm the author, so I get to thank whomever I want.

Ana Maria Garcia, gracias por tu amor y amabilidad.

And finally, a big thanks to my parents: to my father, Neil Puller, for taking such a profound interest in every step of this journey and always getting so excited when it was time to take another one; and to my mother, Deborah Goldberg, who I promised to thank first and last when I win my first Tony Award. Still working on it, Mom!

J. S. PULLER is a playwright and author. She has a master's degree in elementary education and a bachelor's degree in theatre from Northwestern University. She is an award-winning member of the American Alliance for Theatre and Education and has done research on the social-emotional benefits of arts education, with the University of Chicago Consortium on School Research. In addition to *The Lost Things Club*, she is the author of *Captain Superlative*, her debut novel, and several published plays, including *Women Who Weave*, *Perseus and Medusa—It's All Greek to Me!*, and *The Death of Robin Hood*. When not writing, she can usually be found in the theatre. She lives in Chicago. She invites you to visit her at pullerwrites.wordpress.com, on Facebook @puller.writes, and on Twitter @pullerwrites.